RENEGADE'S REVENGE!

Thirteen pairs of eyes watched the small contingent ride out of Fort Thompson. They belonged to Big Foot and the rabble he had gathered around him. These twelve constituted the most efficient of the crop of thugs, cutpurses, rollers, and road agents he employed. Three were black, former slaves who had drifted West and ended up in a life of crime. The others, who all had some degree of Indian blood, were short of temper and devoid of moral principles. Ony the brute size and ferocity of Big Foot kept them in line.

They looked hungrily at the small band of horsemen with eyes that gleamed with blood-lust. Big Foot pointed out Eli Holten.

"That one," he growled. "We follow, and when the time is right, *we kill him.*"

VISIT THE WILD WEST
with Zebra Books

SPIRIT WARRIOR   (1795, $2.50)
by G. Clifton Wisler
The only settler to survive the savage Indian attack was a
little boy. Although raised as a red man, every man was his
enemy when the two worlds clashed — but he vowed no
man would be his equal.

IRON HEART   (1736, $2.25)
by Walt Denver
Orphaned by an Indian raid, Ben vowed he'd never rest
until he'd brought death to the Arapahoes. And it wasn't
long before they came to fear the rider of vengeance they
called . . . *Iron Heart*.

THE DEVIL'S BAND   (1903, $2.25)
by Robert McCaig
For Pinkerton detective Justin Lark, the next assignment
was the most dangerous of his career. To save his beautiful
young client's sisters and brother, he had to face the mean-
est collection of hardcases he had ever seen.

KANSAS BLOOD   (1775, $2.50)
by Jay Mitchell
The Barstow Gang put a bullet in Toby Markham, but they
didn't kill him. And when the Barstow's threatened a
young girl named Lonnie, Toby was finished with running
and ready to start killing.

SAVAGE TRAIL   (1594, $2.25)
by James Persak
Bear Paw seemed like a harmless old Indian — until he stole
the nine-year-old son of a wealthy rancher. In the weeks of
brutal fighting the guns of the White Eyes would clash
with the ancient power of the red man.

*Available wherever paperbacks are sold, or order direct from the
Publisher. Send cover price plus 50¢ per copy for mailing and
handling to Zebra Books, Dept. 2149, 475 Park Avenue South,
New York, N.Y. 10016. Residents of New York, New Jersey and
Pennsylvania must include sales tax. DO NOT SEND CASH.*

#25

THE SCOUT

ROCKY MOUNTAIN BALL

BY BUCK GENTRY

ZEBRA BOOKS
KENSINGTON PUBLISHING CORP.

Special acknowledgements to Mark K. Roberts

ZEBRA BOOKS

are published by

Kensington Publishing Corp.
475 Park Avenue South
New York, NY 10016

First printing: August 1987

Printed in the United States of America

It's with great pleasure that I dedicate this volume of the adventures of Eli Holten to my cousin, Clifford Collins, of Wichita, Kansas, on condition that he promises not to beat me too badly at golf.

BG—

Foreword

In the effort to bring together into one exciting story the lives of two warrior chiefs, Joseph of the Nez Percé and Crazy Horse of the Oglala, it has been necessary to take some liberties with time, events, and place. Nevertheless, these dynamic events did in fact occur between April and October of the same year. If the reader finds himself bogged down with too rapid or too slow changes of time, the author asks he or she bear with it, in order to enjoy the powerful drama that unfolds. It has not been my purpose to be a chronicler of history, but rather to entertain. For those who might wish it, the author recommends that those who want to learn more obtain and read *The Flight of the Nez Percé,* by Mark H. Brown, University of Nebraska Press, Lincoln, Nebraska, 1967, and *Crazy Horse: The Strange Man of the Oglalas,* by Mari Sandoz, Hastings House, New York, 1970.

BG—

Chapter 1

Lips.

Soft and fluttery, like the wings of tiny birds, the lips moved over his warm, moist skin. Steam rose from the waist-deep water that surrounded him in the big copper bath. One pair of lips found his right nipple, the other his left, and a low-power jolt of pleasure spread slowly through his body. How could it be otherwise, Eli Holten wondered, after nearly an all-day session of wildness with the two delightful redheads?

His cool gray eyes studied the auburn mop of Doreen Thorne's thick hair and he singled out the determined technique of her tongue on his flesh from that of her equally engaged carrot-topped sister, Malissa, on the opposite side. They were good, Eli had to admit. Alone or together, they provided everything, if not a little more, that a man could desire. The winter months, through which he had recuperated at the Thorne homestead, had gently metamorphosed to spring; the marvelous ministrations of Doreen and Malissa had dulled the sense of passing time and changing seasons.

But now, although he was fully recovered, the delightful pair had almost been his undoing. Matthew Thorne, now eighteen, had found the love of his life and moved to a home of his own. Old Gabe, along with Mark, Luke John, and Peter, had gone off "a'lookin' " for a few days, leaving Eli as a guest of Doreen, Malissa, Samantha, Susanna, Helen, and Paul. That had been two days ago. The bedstead antics had begun the first night, with a passionate visit from Doreen. They had not let up since. Following breakfast that morning, Doreen had announced that she and her sister would provide Eli's entertainment together.

For a while, his stamina had held. Eli Holten, chief scout of the Twelfth U.S. Cavalry, had not become legend among the ladies of the frontier by saintly abstinence. His exploits came from the substance of myths. His prowess was Herculean. At least, until two eager, energetic, and phenomenally lusty girls in their late teens, had combined their talents to reduce him to a limpid, sighing puddle of flesh. Wet, questing fingers found his semierect organ and began manipulating it.

"Ooh," Malissa lamented. "He's not doin' anything."

"Ummm," Doreen responded. "You gotta try harder." Giggling, she cupped the scout's scrotum.

"Wel-l-l-l, that ain't helpin' much," Malissa observed a moment later.

Mischieviously, the girls exchanged glances. "I know what he needs," Doreen decreed.

"Yeah. We'll have to give him a *real* surprise."

"Exactly, 'Lissa. Close your eyes, Eli," Doreen prompted. "Real tight, now. And no fair peekin', till we tell you to."

"Want me to cross my heart?" Eli sighed, resigned to the game.

Long, silent moments passed. Eli's sensitive hearing made out the whisper of cloth. Were they getting

10

dressed for some reason? And some heavy female breathing. Were they relieving each other's needs for lack of energy on his part? A soft, happy squeal came close-by his ears. Then the pressure of lips against his, tasting of horehound. A tongue, hard, sweet, and persistent, stabbing in and out of his mouth. It moved down over his chin, across his throat, onto his chest.

Another set of lips, tasting of lemon, and a tongue. Now fingers, light and rapid, caressed, explored, progressed downward. Wild sensations awakened within him and his mighty phallus rose above the water's surface.

"Eeek!" a high voice exclaimed.

"Aaaaah," sighed another.

Hands found his rigid device, one, two, three, four. In a firm, skillful grip, they stroked him. Warm, moist lips closed over the burning tip of his mighty lance. Eli wanted desperately to open his eyes and see how they had managed another performance out of his depleted body. Yet he sensed that the guessing at who did what might be a large part of his new arousal.

Soft petals nibbled at the rock-firm shaft. Another pair joined. And another. *Another?* How?

"Don't look," came Doreen's urgent voice from near his waist.

"Raise up, raise up," Malissa coaxed.

Eli elevated his hips and felt a splash as two legs entered the water. Warm, silky flesh brushed his skin. More disturbance of the bath sloshed a wave over the side. A soft grunt sounded above him as a hot, wet tightness surrounded his throbbing penis. With deliberate slowness the elastic tunnel ingested more of his maleness. Three sets of lips went to work around the base of his pillar.

Three?

"Ooooh . . . it's . . . won-der-ful!" a sweet, passion-thickened voice exulted.

"Hurry, silly. I want my turn," an identical voice responded.

Eli's eyes flew open. Mystery solved. There were now *four* lovely, naked pink ladies administering to him. Doreen and Malissa had been joined by their twin sisters, Samantha or Susanna, swayed her hips from side to side in an effort to absorb more of his pulsing member, while the other, along with Dorie and 'Lissa, slathered its base with their tongues.

"See," Malissa took time off to taunt. "Told you we could get you goin' again."

Eli gulped and fought to control his startled reaction. "Are you out of your minds? Get them out of here. Th-they're only children."

"Be fifteen in three days," Susanna or Samantha retorted as she impaled herself on more of his turgid shaft.

"You weren't fair to us last winter, but we're makin' up for it." Samantha or Susanna pouted.

Eli at last managed to get into the conversation. "The point it, you're *not fifteen now!*"

"Nine's the marryin' age where we come from," Malissa informed him.

"You're not there, you're here," Eli protested, his passion waning.

"Here it's twelve," Samantha and Susanna smugly told him.

"Paw checked it out," his eager rider went on alone. " 'We Thornes are law-abidin' folk. So, before you young 'uns run wild out here, we want to make sure there's no statute again' it,' he told us. So there."

Eli gaped. Before he could muster further protests, the door flew open and Paul entered, grinning at the

12

sight, though with his brow furrowed by a frown.

"Y'all had better get straightened up. Rider comin' this way."

With wild squeals, the girls flew about like a covey of frightened quail. Paul remained until Eli growled at him. "Get out there and delay him a while, kid. Do it!"

When everyone had returned to clothing and the tub slid behind a hanging curtain, Doreen assumed a demure expression, eyes properly downcast, and opened the door. "Won't you come in, stranger?"

"Thank you, ma'am."

The stranger turned out to be in uniform. Eli Holten immediately recognized it as bad news.

"Are you Eli Holten, chief scout from Fort Rawlins?"

"I am," Eli admitted to the fresh-faced young trooper. "What can I do for you?"

"Colonel Miles's compliments, sir, and would you join him at Fort Thompson?"

"I can assume that the colonel has wired to General Corrington for orders to that effect, soldier?"

A small grin lifted the corners of the young man's mouth, though his eyes remained fixed on the bountiful display of feminine pulchritude. "I couldn't say, sir, though I'd imagine so. It's regulation."

Eli sighed and made a helpless gesture. "Then, I suppose, we'll have to end our pleasant reunion somewhat early," he directed to the Thornes. "I'll pack my gear and be right with you," he told the messenger.

"Uh . . . wha-what?"

The soldier's attention snapped back suddenly from the scintillating vision of the strawberry-haired, barely nubial twins, who glowed with the special vividness that comes only from recent sexual excita-

13

tion. All of them, he realized, had it, except for the youngest girl and the boy. He examined the tall, lean frame of the blond scout with new respect. *All four of them*? *At one time*? Awh, it couldn't be.

"Never mind," Eli answered gently.

Private Danny Neeley twitched with suppressed excitement as he walked out from the cantonment area of Fort Thompson. He'd heard of it for a long time now. Half the fellas in his platoon had gotten a little. Several claimed it to be the best they'd ever encountered.

"You'll get a good time, that's for sure," his best friend, Ed Shields, had guaranteed.

Danny Neeley wasn't exactly sure what a good time might be. At nineteen, his worldly experience amounted to little indeed. Oh, there had been some hugging and snuggling and kissy-face with Mary Sue back behind the schoolhouse when they were in the upper grades together. And a hurried, furtive coupling with a Hooker's Girl in Jefferson City at the end of his induction training at Jefferson Barracks, Missouri. Neither had been fully satisfactory. Now the rigid bulge in the front of his trousers urged him on to discover if this "good time" would be any better than the others. She said she'd meet him at the edge of the stand of cottonwoods to the east of the fort.

Beyond, Danny knew, was a small stream and the endless stretch of the Dakota Territory prairie. Far off lay the Black Hills and beyond them, some indefinable where, civilization. Right now his attention remained riveted on the prospect of satisfying a demanding urge. Only another twenty yards and he'd find it.

Then she was before him, all flashing white teeth,

14

big, dark eyes and shiny long hair. "You come," she said in a throaty, thrilling voice.

"I, ah . . . yes."

"Don't be shy," she coaxed. "Come, follow me."

Deep into the grove stood a small teepee, its unpainted sides declaring to the knowledgeable the poverty and low status of the owner. A curl of blue smoke above the variable vent proclaimed refuge from the sharp edge of spring wind.

Behind her smiling, welcoming mask, she studied him in his uniform. Regulations required that anyone leaving the post wear a sidearm and carry his rifle or carbine. This young, nervous soldier had followed orders to the letter. He looked so like a boy, she thought as she took his hand and led him into the snug interior. Shy. Not like the others. She felt something within her go out to him. He must have felt it too, for he squeezed her hand and gazed fondly down on her. Somewhere among the cottonwoods, a clear creek made musical sounds as it burbled over smooth rocks.

She gazed up at the lanky teenager and he took her in his arms. "Pay me now," she demanded.

Jerkily, Danny Neeley extracted the two silver dollars from his trousers pocket and laid them on her palm. She gave him a fleeting, dimpled smile and made the money disappear into a small purse tied at her waist. She loosened the belt that supported her bag and let it drop to her sleeping robes.

"Do you want to undress me?"

"Ummmm, ah, er, wh-why not?" Danny responded brokenly.

With all the bumbling ineptitude of the inexperienced, he fumbled at the hem of her skirt, at last drawing it upward. "Start with this," she instructed. "With my blouse."

Danny flushed at his betrayal of lack of finesse and did as he had been told. His efforts were rewarded with the sight of two large, firm, pertly uptilted mounds. Dark, nearly maroon nipples began to swell at the soft caress of the breeze. Danny moaned softly and feared he might ejaculate in his trousers. Shakily, he reached out and brushed those astounding breasts with his fingertips.

"Take off th' shirt," she directed.

Danny drew his dark blue woolen uniform blouse from the waistband of his trousers and yanked it over his head. The prairie breeze from the open flap ran on tiny feet over his pale white skin. He shivered slightly and she stepped close to him. Her arms circled his neck and drew him to her. Her breasts touched his chest as they started to kiss. Then one hand left his neck and dropped low between them. Deftly she opened his fly and brought out his rigid, quivering organ.

Slowly she stroked it and Danny recoiled reflexively from the intensely pleasurable sensation it created. For a moment he feared he might explode his sap before they got to the main business of the afternoon. A soft moan of passion rose from deep inside him.

Danny Neeley's audible ardor changed to a gurgling groan of mortal despair when someone grabbed his hair from behind and yanked back on his head, slid a wide, heavy blade into his right kidney, then jerked it free and whipped it across his throat, expertly cutting it from ear to ear. Blood geysered. Danny shook and trembled; his erection wilted to a wrinkled finger-length of pink flesh. Eyes wide at the rush of his very spirit through the gaping wound in his throat, he could do nothing but stare horrified at the smiling girl who danced back away from the spurt of his life force, her passion-swollen breasts now splashed with hot crimson. Both hands clutched uselessly to his throat, Danny Neeley sank to his knees. He swayed there for a moment, then fell onto his left side.

Before the pair departed, they erased all sign of the teepee and deprived Danny of a small sum of money, his service revolver, carbine, and ammunition.

Chapter 2

"There's trouble from here to the Pacific Coast," Colonel Nelson A. Miles informed Eli Holten when the scout reported in at Fort Thompson. "General Howard has more than his hands full with the Nez Percé. They've been balking over a move to the Wallowa Valley, not that I blame them. It's not the best of their former lands and is infested with riffraff the vigilance committees ran out of nearby settlements. That's only a start. The Sioux we rounded up are but a handful of those believed to still be out. In particular, Crazy Horse."

"I know him rather well," Eli said dryly. "If you expect to get him to go on a reservation voluntarily, you have a surprise coming."

"Do I, indeed? My purpose in summoning you here was to have you act as an emissary to talk Crazy Horse into bringing his people to the reservation. I'm aware that you and he are more than sometime acquaintances. Please, tell me about him."

Eli leaned back in the uncomfortable camp chair and laced his fingers behind the back of his head. He eyed the bottle of bourbon Colonel Miles sat on the table and longed for the subtle, wood-cask flavor of Frank Corrington's superb brandy. His blue-gray eyes clouded slightly as he let the years slough off and he began to relate his knowledge of the Oglala war chief to Nelson Miles.

"He was called Curly as a boy. He had light, curly hair and was small for his age. When he was about twelve, his father, also called Crazy Horse, gave him the name His Horse Looking. I met him at my first Sun Dance. I'd been living with the Oglala band in which he has several relatives, I was not quite fifteen at the time, he was I'd guess a couple of months past his seventeenth birthday." Holten paused and moistened his vocal cords with some of Miles's whiskey. Not bad, he decided. Definitely better than he had expected.

"There was a fight that spring against some Paiutes, whom the Sioux call the People Who Live in Grass Houses. Curly participated in the final big battle, when the Paiutes came after the raiders. He went out and collected two neglected scalps from fallen Paiutes, right under their guns, got shot in the leg for it, and later was given his name Crazy Horse by his father for his brave deeds. Then, in high summer, the Sun Dance was held. He watched me dance with the *Wambli Gleska* society. I recall him distinctly. I'd been encouraging *Pisko*, who you will recall from last winter's campaign. I shuffled and danced and played an eagle wing-bone whistle, and watched him watching me. His eyes seemed to penetrate right into my skull. I grew thirsty and tired and began to stagger and stumble like a drunk. Still Crazy Horse sat there with the honored guests and watched me.

"Somehow," Eli returned briefly to the present and sipped more whiskey, as though sharing that mighty sunburned thirst of the past, "he infused me with his courage. He wasn't a big man. Always small in stature since a boy. But somehow he was big enough for both of us that day. I had no idea then that the next day, the big, final ceremony of the Sun Dance, before the feast, that Crazy Horse would accept the wooden skewers through his chest and take up the thongs to dance the *wiwanyag wacipi*, the sun gazing. After that, and the enormous feast, where I ate like a starved dog, I found myself a barely pubescent fourteen-year-old white boy, whose greatest hero was an Oglala warrior hardly three years older. In no time at all I made myself completely Indian. Or at least, that's how I saw it."

Holten relaxed a moment, refreshed his whiskey glass, and lighted a long, thin cigar. He shook his head, unsure why he made these intimate revelations to the black-bearded, stern-faced army officer across from him.

"Later some bad blood developed between Crazy Horse and Red Cloud and his kin. It was over a woman, of all things. Since boyhood, Crazy Horse had a bit of, ah, I guess you'd say a crush on Red Cloud's niece. When the time came and Red Cloud and the girl's father gave Black Buffalo Woman in marriage to No Water, the girl and Crazy Horse sort of considered that a mistake had been made and set about correcting it."

"In other words, he stole another man's wife?"

"Colonel, that's a bit simplistic for dealing with Crazy Horse. He's the most complex person I've ever known. The comeuppance was that No Water came after his woman. He had a six-gun concealed in the back of his waistband and went storming into Crazy Horse's lodge. Crazy Horse started for him with a knife in his hand and Little Big Man, who next to his 'brother by choice,' He Dog, had been Crazy Horse's closest friend since early childhood, reached out and held Crazy Horse by one arm. It was to prevent him from committing the unpardonable sin among the Sioux of killing one of their own kind. Little thanks he got for it, because No Water carried out his murderous intentions and shot Crazy Horse in the face.

"He fled, naturally, with Little Big Man on his trail. Meanwhile, Crazy Horse lay like death in his lodge. All the medicine in the world wouldn't save him. Yet, by a miracle and a little thoughtful probing and cleaning up by the medicine man, he did survive. It came out later that the cartridge had been only half charged to save powder. In the meantime, Little Big Man never did catch up with No Water. He returned in, as he considered it, disgrace. When Crazy Horse recovered enough he praised and rewarded his friend. The failed assassination only made more hard feelings between Red Cloud's Bad Faces clan and Crazy Horse. Little Big Man became Crazy Horse's most dedicated follower and a steadfast supporter. More like a fanatic worshiper, if you ask me. Little Big Man has no love of agencies, and through that, you can be sure Crazy Horse will not either."

"That's quite some tale," Miles commented dryly, refilling their glasses. "Surely, from all I've heard, an appeal can be made to Crazy Horse's wisdom. He is a smart man, I've been told."

"More than 'smart' by most lights. Brilliant might better fit. He thinks things through before acting and no one, not even Little Big Man, can tell what belief or moral standing or whim dictates the way Crazy Horse will react. To say he's not predictable is an understatement. To say he's inconsistent and whimsical is not to know the man at all. He's . . . as I said before, complex."

"Your, ah, description would make a rather good

tribute."

"I respect Crazy Horse. I used to idolize him. But one thing I never do is underrate him," Eli responded mildly to the goad.

"Ummmm. What about now? How do his people feel about him and he about them?"

"He's a mystic. A magic warrior who is never hit by the enemy's bullets unless held by one of his own people. A wounded Sioux held him when the Ute bullet struck. He can ride any horse and tame it with words. Or at least the Sioux believe so. He and Red Cloud's people are still on the outs. I would never consider attempting to talk him in if he were to be put on the same agency with the Brule and Red Cloud's Bad Face clan."

"I, ah, see. You've given me a lot to digest, Mr. Holten. Enough, I think, that we should adjourn until tomorrow morning. Thank you for your help. I hope Fort Thompson, primitive as it is, provides you with some comforts."

Holten produced a warm smile. "I'm sure it will."

Big Foot watched the firm, round, delightful mounds of the youthful teamster's behind as they bunched and swayed under the split riding skirt, and slobbered. Should be easy to roll in his blanket, he thought as tobacco juice ran down his huge, rocklike chin. Willin', too, he convinced himself. Why else would a female like Jenny Blanchard take on a man's job? Get to go lots of places and give it away to lots of fellers, that's what. Like him, for instance. Big Foot pushed himself away from the undressed log front of the sutler's store and started toward the young woman, who effortlessly handled the hundred-pound burlap bag of white beans.

"Let me give you a hand, honey. Pretty little thing like you shouldn't be strugglin' . . ."

"Get out of my way, you lunk. I can handle it quite well without you."

"I'll bet you can," Big Foot grunted. "Reckon you can handle 'bout near anything. Even my eight hot inches," he sneered in addition.

While he leered and spoke tauntingly, Big Foot reached out with one gigantic paw and cupped a round cheek of her bottom. The bag fell to the ground, and in a blur he failed to identify in time, Jenny whipped out a trim belt knife at her left side and shoved it about a quarter of an inch into his muscle-ridged gut.

"Back off, you 'breed bastard," Jenny growled.

Big Foot did, with alacrity. He also slapped the blade out of her hand and swung a powerful arm, backhanding her so violently she went to her knees. The sound attracted Eli Holten's attention as he stepped from the partially constructed headquarters building. It also attracted something else.

With a wild bellow of outrage, Liver Eating Johnson dashed into the scene, fists balled, face scarlet with rage and a curse for Big Foot on his lips. His first punch set Big Foot's right ear to ringing, a trickle of blood running from torn skin. The second rocked the giant backward. Then the fight got down to earnest.

At six foot eight, Big Foot remained half a head smaller than the Liver Eater, though a good many years younger. He sweated and grunted while they traded blows, any one of which would have felled a lesser man. With each devastating punch he grated out his words.

"You . . . ain't . . . got . . . any call . . . to be . . . buttin' in . . . Liver Eater. Keep . . . yer . . . nose

23

outta . . . . my business . . . with . . . my girl."

"Your girl, you mangy half-breed lump of pig shit? Your girl? Not by a long fucking way!" Johnson retorted, his mouth, as usual, filled with blue, sharp-edged obscenities. "You ain't got the decency of a dog shittin' on the church steps."

By this time, Eli Holten had arrived. The fists flew wildly. Liver Eater faked a kick to Big Foot's groin, then crossed the grimy 'breed's eyes with a knuckle-splitter left to the center of his forehead. Then he shifted quickly and delivered the kick anyway.

"Even money on the 'breed stranger?"

Eli spared a glance at the dapper figure of a soldier he dimly recognized as a gambler and loan shark from the winter campaign.

"Gimme three to five on the old man." Eli demanded, returning to the fight.

Big Foot reeled, gulped, and recovered. He came on, bent low, bull head set to ram into Liver Eating Johnson's belly. Liver Eater sidestepped and walloped Big Foot with a savage right to the other ear. Bells tolled for the mixed-race idler. He snorted and shook his head and came on again. He locked his arms around Johnson and began to squeeze.

"Done, nobody gets out of that bastard's hold." The gambler's tight grin was wasted for lack of an audience.

Muscles bulged and arms quivered as Big Foot applied pressure. Open-palmed, Liver Eater popped both of Big Foot's ears. The bells turned to chimes and shrill silver whistles. Big Foot gagged and relaxed his hold slightly. Then he butted the big Liver Eater in the belly.

Howling, Johnson began stamping up and down on the hard-packed ground. Each upstroke drove his knee into Big Foot's chest. While he worked on his opponent in this manner, he also drummed on his head with both fists. Black spots formed as Big Foot tightened up. Johnson began to feel a bit of drag from his age. He only hit harder.

Blood ran from both ears and Big Foot's mouth. He sagged and the hard-driving knees banged into his chest, then his chin, and at last his nose. Cartilage crunched and he staggered free. Liver Eating Johnson came after him. Kicks and punches landed in strategic spots and Big Foot uttered a wavering moan before he plunged face first onto the ground. Johnson stood panting for a moment, then closed in and used a solid, lifting kick to roll his felled opponent over.

He whipped out his knife and slit through Big Foot's wide leather belt, parting the thin cloth of his shirt next. Liver Eater dropped to his knees and prepared to plunge the big blade deep into flesh to get at his favorite delicacy, when Eli stepped in close and grabbed the wrist of Johnson's knife hand.

"Now, that's mighty antisocial of you, Liver Eater," Eli purred in his most persuasive voice.

"Holten? Eli Holten?" Johnson inquired through the red haze of his rage.

"The same. Now you know, Liver Eater, that the Army can and probably will muster up the resolution to hunt you down and hang you for murder, if not cannibalism, if you go through with that. What's nice and tasty, given a little salt, to you is downright disgusting to them."

"Awh, damn it all to hell, it ain't fair, Eli. This piss-ant done insulted a fine lady, he did. *Put his hand on her*, he did. Defiled her pure soul. I decided to kick the livin' shit outta him for it. Now you come along and spoil it all."

"No other way about it, Liver Eater. You cut that

25

'breed and the Army will make gallows bait out of you."

"You damn sure on that?"

"I am."

"So am I," Jenny added her voice to Eli's as a clincher. "You saved me, that was more than wonderful, but it surely was enough. No need to shed blood . . . ah, that is, *more* blood."

"Aawh, well then, I guess I better get up an' let him go."

Which he did, delivering a solid stomp to Big Foot's face in the process. "Good seein' ya again, Eli. Can I buy you a drink?"

"Not right now, thanks. Just got in. Later tonight, though, I'm game."

"See ya at the sutler's then."

Grinning, Johnson staggered off to recuperate. He'd not, the scout knew, bother to wash up.

Eli held his three-dollar stake in his left hand and extended the right to the gambler.

"Should have let the old man finish. That would have been a show worth five bucks." The dapper little soldier flinched from the look in Eli's blue eyes and handed over the cash.

"I'm grateful to him and all," Jenny said by way of introduction, "but downwind he's mighty gamy."

"That he is. I'm Eli Holton, scout for the Twelfth Cavalry."

"Hello, Eli. I'm Jenny. Jenny Blanchard. I do contract hauling."

Eli gave the small, curvaceous, sweet-faced blonde a long speculative and contemplative look. Up and down, then up again to firm, well-formed breasts that poked out the front of her paisley shirt. A slow grin spread.

"I'm more than a little pleased to meet you, Jenny.

26

Colonel Miles said he hoped I'd find something comforting on the post. I think I have."

"Fine," came through Jenny's inviting smile. "Now, I'll buy you a drink for sparing that disgusting hulk's miserable life. I can't abide killing. Especially of the cold-blooded kind." She turned a withering glance on the gambler, who crawled off to locate more promising action.

"I'll accept, on condition I get to buy the second round."

"Done."

Taking her arm over his, Eli Holten walked Jenny toward the sutler's place, his heart thumping merrily and a grin of pure delight spread wide across his sun-browned face.

Chapter 3

Dust rose in the clear September air. Churned up by two hundred forty hoofs, it lingered as a moving miasma over the solid brown, spotted, and black hides of the cattle. At the head of the small herd, Walter Lehman looked back over his shoulder and pursed his lips in satisfaction.

"They ain't much," he commented to the man on his left. "But fed up, they'll bring a good price."

"Yeah, and we got 'em cheap enough."

The stubble-chinned drover's remark brought a sharp bark of laughter from Lehman. His broad face, marked off in neat symmetries of wide-spaced, soft brown eyes, vertical slash of straight-edged nose, and generous, thin-lipped mouth, wore the perpetual sun and weather tanning that would never fade. He had spent years on the frontier, yet none so lucrative as the last two. Walter Lehman's association with Duncan McAllister provided each with what he needed. Not one to question a promising enterprise, Lehman had so far given his utmost to the partnership.

Which resulted in the Box M ranch prospering beyond expectations. Sixty head of new cattle would increase profit considerably. He liked the jingle of money in his pocket. The soft rustle of crisp, new large-denomination bills he liked even more.

"We'll head 'em in shortly, Sol," he informed the drover. "By tomorrow this time we can stop long enough to do the branding. Don't pay to have a man's cattle unmarked around these parts."

Solomon Greer produced a crooked smile. "Right you are, boss. Never know when some Injun'll steal 'em, or rustlers take 'em off yer hands, eh? The boys'll be grateful for an early stop. A hot meal ought to improve tempers a mite, I'd say."

"See to it, then," Lehman instructed the granite-jawed, gray-eyed foreman.

Jenny's offer to buy a drink turned out to include unloading the last supplies from her wagon. She managed the addition without the slightest bit of artifice. Holten couldn't help but admire her open manipulation. After each had purchased a round, Jenny suggested a hot meal for supper. Eli readily agreed.

It turned out she hadn't in mind the hastily constructed, wooden-walled, tent-roofed eatery next to the sutler's store, where one could get buffalo and antelope steak, boiled onions and potatoes, fried squaw bread, and duff pudding. After unhitching her team and putting them in the civilian corral, she led the scout to a small, sturdy cabin.

"My place," she announced simply. "Won't you come in, kind sir?"

Grinning, Eli entered. The place was a disaster area. Clothing hung on pegs, or lay tossed in corners. A layer of dust covered chairs, table, and a four-lid cast-iron cooking stove. Jenny waved a hand negligently.

"I only use this place when I'm on this end of a

freighting job. Don't it look awful?"

Tactfully, Eli refrained from comment. Jenny took his hat and light whipcord jacket and hung them on a free peg. She had not yet disposed of hers and didn't do so until she had completed a thorough rummage through drawers and cabinets. She came up with two stained, chipped china cups and a partly filled bottle of Old Overholt.

"Start the fire," she instructed as she doffed her hat and coat. "I'll pour the rye."

Eli found kindling ready on a fresh, fluffy pile of white ashes and touched a match to the slender strips of wood. They blazed readily and he added larger lengths from a bucket to one side. Jenny poured two generous fingers of whiskey into each cup and handed one to her guest. She raised her eyes to lock her gaze on his, giving her lovely, heart-shaped face a demure cast.

"To a long, warm friendship," she toasted.

"To us," Eli added.

Cup rims clinked together and Jenny polished off her drink in a long swallow. She set aside the cup and ferreted out a small tin bucket. As she headed for the door, she called over her shoulder to Eli.

"Be right back. Sit and relax."

She returned twenty minutes later with a foaming pail of milk. "Mary O'Dancy, the provost sergeant's wife, keeps a milk cow," she explained. From behind her back, she produced a freshly plucked chicken. "I thought we'd want cream gravy with fried chicken and biscuits."

Eli shook his head in astonishment. This calico-and-leather-clad husky young female taking on domestic airs gave him a great deal of pleasure. He rose and added fuel to the firebox.

"Anything I can do to help?"

"No, not really. Only . . . to be here. To eat with me and . . ." Jenny let it drift.

Holton could not overlook the warm invitation in her eyes. He came to where she worked on the chicken in a granite basin. Standing close he circled her trim waist with his arms, fingers clasped together on her flat belly, and rested his chin on her shoulder. She shivered slightly, then turned her head and gave him an approving smile.

Following a most tasty and satisfying meal, Eli Holton sat near the warmth of the stove in a rocking chair and sipped coffee laced with sugar and good rye whiskey. Jenny did the dishes. Soft yellow light filled the room from a kerosene lamp with a hand-painted glass shade. After a few probing questions, Jenny got the broad-shouldered, usually taciturn scout to talking about his life on the frontier.

At one point, she burst into a peal of delighted giggles. "I can't picture you as a tow-headed Oglala boy running around in breechcloth and moccasins."

"Well, I did," Eli answered defensively. "When I was a kid, I was small for my age. I looked more twelve than fourteen when they took me in."

"I don't believe you were ever *small* for your age . . . not in any part of you," Jenny answered in a low, husky voice.

"It didn't last long," Eli went on, ignoring the blatant invitation. When he was certain and ready, he'd take the lead in *that* direction. "On a diet of buffalo, instead of boiled cabbage and spongy potatoes, I began to shoot up fast. In late spring, even the Sioux traded with tribes who raised Indian corn. It's a lot better for your teeth and innards than what white folks eat."

"Ummm. I can see that well enough. Like I said at the sutler's this afternoon, it ain't everyone who can back down Liver Eating Johnson."

"We fought once. To a standstill."

"My! I *am* impressed. You're big, but he'd make near on two of you."

"Well, I have to confess he'd already whipped a damn good man and was a little winded."

"Tell me about the other times. After you left the Oglala?"

Eli recounted more of his history. He told of his time as a bullwhacker for a freighting outfit — one trip. Of drifting for a while, learning the ways of whites again. Then of signing up as a civilian scout for the army. Jenny drew him out on the places he'd been and the Indian campaigns he had participated in. At last he concluded with a probe of his own.

"We've burned up more'n an hour on *me*. A dull subject at best. What about you? How'd you ever become an independent teamster, Jenny?"

Jenny made a face, her nose crinkling into an impertinent, uptilted stub. "Oh, there's not a lot to tell. I'm free, white, and twenty-one. Over by a bit, truth to tell. My father, Gaston Blanchard, was half French-Canadian. He owned a large mercantile in the Lakes Country. Sold and shipped to settlers and Indian reservations around the Great Lakes. His folks had come to this country during England's troubles with France over sixty years ago. I'm the oldest of three girls, with three brothers older and two younger." She rose to top off Eli's cup again.

"Just coffee, this time, please," he requested.

"Coming up. Now, where was I? Oh, yes, my undistinguished girlhood. It was, you know. You may have been a slow bloomer, but I wasn't. I grew up fast. Too fast for being a girl, if you know what I mean. My father had me doing chores at eight that my brother two years older couldn't handle. I was big and strong at about twelve, folks used to tell my father what a sturdy son he had in me. Resent it? Hell, yes, I did. But I learned to harness teams, load and tie down wagons . . . I was driving the light rig for town deliveries at eleven."

"When did you ever have time for being a girl?" Eli inquired.

"I didn't . . . much. I left dollies and dresses behind at the age of eight. I had stuffed animals to play with, but they were horses and mules and some beautifully hand-carved wagon models with every detail on the mules and harness perfect. Father used to drill me on the names of parts. Inside I *felt* like a girl, but outside I acted like a boy. It made father happy. At least I thought so. My sisters, all fluffy and crinkly in crinoline and lace, made my life miserable. When we were small, they'd go around wiggling a finger in front of their dresses, ah, down below, and calling me Jimmy instead of Jenny. Father caught them at it one time and blistered their bottoms good. I think that deep inside they resented me because I got to do all the things they didn't. Boy things. I, ah, even went skinny-dipping once in a while with my brothers and their friends."

"And?"

"They treated me like one of them. At least until the lumps showed up. Then I got shy and they got much more interested. Oh, I didn't lose my virtue to a panting thirteen-year-old on a mud bank along a creek or anything like that. I kept it until that glorious, golden summer night when I was fourteen. Then . . . then it just seemed like the right thing to do. Does that make any sense to you?"

Grinning, the scout reached out in a gesture that brought Jenny to his lap in the rocker. "Yes, it does. It makes you sound like a very determined, strong-willed, self-controlled young lady. Were you still driving team for your father?"

"No. Not by then." Jenny shifted position and kissed Eli lightly on the forehead. "I'd discovered music. The piano. Father gladly paid for the lessons. And no, my piano teacher *didn't* seduce me. I fell in love for the first time that year. With a boy who also took lessons from the same teacher. He was shy and sensitive, with long, slender fingers and an almost reverent love for music. I . . . I'm afraid it was I who seduced him."

"I'd call that rather enterprising," Eli commented in a tone of approval.

"Eli! I thought I would shock you."

"You didn't, Jenny. What you're doing is arousing me even more than your looks and your sweet kindness. Much more of this and I won't leave here to find a place for the night."

"I, ah, kinda hoped you wouldn't," Jenny responded, nearly an appeal.

Eli kissed her soundly then. A long, heated buss that left their lips tingling and hearts pounding. Jenny leaned back her head and Eli kissed a throbbing pulse in her neck. She made small murmuring sounds of delight and he ventured further, to cup and knead her firm, globular breasts. She squirmed against his erection and brought forth a low, throaty chuckle.

"Oh, oh, Eli, I like this. I—I feel so . . . at home. A home of my own, I mean. And a man of m— Don't mind me. I tend to get carried away. A tough-talking lady teamster doesn't attract many gentle, loving men. At best it's women-haters like Big Foot, who wants to take out his mad, but shrinks from a more ladylike victim."

"You're quite incisive," Eli complimented, while he

34

worked on her shirt buttons.

The middle one, between her breasts, slipped free and a robust, delicately pink set of mammary delights popped forth. Eli bent his head to nuzzle them. Jenny sighed.

"Eli, I think I'm going to be made happy tonight. Very, very happy."

With only a small grunt of effort, Eli stood with Jenny in his arms. He carried her to the cast-iron bedstead and lowered her lithe body to the covers. While she watched with far-from-calm detachment, he removed his clothes. Jenny gasped when she saw the white slashes, puckered cicatrices, and angry red lumps of his many wounds.

"Y-you didn't tell me about those," she breathed out.

"Surely you don't want to know about every one?" Eli deprecated.

"I want to kiss each one and make it well and to go away."

"You can try, Jenny, though I don't feel you'll have much success."

Eli slid out of his trousers and revealed the massive, rigid dimensions of his maleness. Jenny's lips trembled at the sight and she wet them with a pale pink tongue tip. Although by no means an innocent, her experience had been small and limited to only three lovers, and one of those so long ago and only a boy a year older than herself. However could she handle something so—so *manly*? Eli knelt at the bedside and began to remove her boots and the split riding skirt.

Jenny shivered with delight. His big, rough hands on her smooth flesh sent waves of wondrous sensation through her. She sensed the sudden release and heavy, wet flow that made her ready to receive his bounty. Still slightly afrighted at the massive size of him, she squeaked in startled pleasure when Eli began to kiss her body.

Soft lips nuzzled her in-curved waist, worked up over the slight mound of her hard stomach muscles, and settled in the fine, white hairs of her navel. His tongue stabbed and she wriggled with happiness. Then Eli moved on, covering her belly, chest, and tingling breasts with amorous kisses. Desperately she reached out to him and encircled his burning shaft. Eli moaned his own enjoyment as she began to squeeze and stroke him. His fingers parted the sparse blonde thatch that covered her blossoming cleft and found a way within. Involuntarily she thrust her hips upward to receive his attentions more fully. Time and reality seemed to jink askew and freeze out of focus. Her urgent plea echoed over and over in her head through that tiny moment of eternity.

"Oh, be quick, beloved. Take me. Take me and make me yours . . ."

Sometime in the early morning hours, Eli got up to add wood to the fire and padded naked back to bed. Like pink-blushed peaches and cream, Jenny's glorious flesh glowed in the moonlight that entered through the top part of a real glass window. Careful not to wake her, Eli slipped back into the goose-down quilts.

Only to have Jenny grasp hungrily at his relaxed member. A few deft squeezes and a clever thumb over the tip roused it to new life. In a flurry of disarrayed covers, she reversed direction and her blond locks brushed over Eli's belly as she lowered her head and closed soft lips over the broad, flat tip of his achingly rigid phallus.

Slowly Jenny worked more of his manhood within the cavity of her mouth. Her ambitious efforts got quick reward when he stiffened his long, rangy body and a tiny grunt burst from his lips. Her own excitement grew the harder she worked, until a blast-furnace heat radiated from her glistening flesh. Bed-springs creaked and the world swayed around the joyful lovers. Unable to prolong the ultimate much longer, Jenny swiftly straddled Eli and impaled herself on the object of her fascination. Surprised and delighted, Eli felt the warm trickle of her love juices escape the normal confines of flesh to form intriguing rivulets down his scrotum.

They galloped together like runaway horses, thundering toward the abyss that beckoned them to oblivion. Gleefully Jenny shrilled as her lusty body peaked and crescendoed. Almost at once the thrilling upsurge began again, so that they crashed harmoniously over the brink in sublime oneness.

"There's no decent place in this raw frontier fort," Jenny said with determination an hour later. "So it's settled. You can move in here with me. I'm taking out another load in a few days, but the place is yours while you're here. Somewhere to hang your hat."

"Rather more than that, I'd say," Eli drawled lazily.

"Whatever. I'll brook no arguments and we'll be dizzily happy when we're together."

"I . . . make it a policy never to argue with a beautiful woman. Consider the invitation accepted. Now, let's get some sleep or I'll look like I've been on a three-day drunk when I see Colonel Miles in the morning."

"Sleep? Who wants to sleep?" Jenny challenged coyly.

Chapter 4

Meadowlarks and chickadees vied with each other to make a nuisance in the early morning air. The regimental trumpeter had just emerged to sound Officers' Call when Eli Holten stepped up the three short treads onto the wide, half-completed porch of headquarters and entered the orderly room.

"Ah, 'tis himself it tis," Sergeant Major Fione Quinlan declared. "T'gen'ral will be seein' ye right of this minute, Mr. Holten."

"Thank you, Quinlan." Eli knocked, entered Miles's office, and removed his hat. "We'll have snow before mid-October," he said by way of greeting.

"Do you always bring bad news, Holten?"

Eli grinned. "It's kind of nice to be the giver, instead of the recipient. General Corrington *always* has bad news for me."

"Sit down. I'm afraid I have more of the same."

Holten took a chair and drew it up close to the desk. "Such as what?"

"I don't have enough trouble, it seems. The regiment's been alerted in the event the pacifying of Joseph's Nez Percé becomes difficult. Crazy Horse is still out there, so are about a thousand Sioux. Now we have another soldier murdered within a quarter mile of the post."

"Another? How long ago?"

"Two others, and all three within two weeks' time. All with their throats cut and stabbed upward from the back, through a kidney. Each trooper had his money, if any, taken, along with his weapons."

"I'm . . . not a detective."

"And too damn bad the army doesn't have some of their own," Miles came back hotly. "I wouldn't have one of those Pinkerton sons of bitches within a hundred miles of my post. Unfortunately, they *are* under government contract and we're supposed to use them when necessary. It would be nice for someone in my command, or . . . someone *attached* to it, to solve this little mystery before I have to resort to calling those mad bombers from Chicago."

"You sound rather bitter toward them," Eli probed.

"Ever hear of the Molly McGuires? During the coal-mining troubles in Pennsylvania. Men beaten and shot to death and imprisoned for wanting survivable working conditions, at the behest of the mine owners, done by Pinkertons. Or what happened to people in southern Missouri? Dispossessed of their homesteads and farms without due process of law, and with no compensation, driven out because they had sympathized with the wrong side in the recent war. A woman had her arm blown off by a dynamite blast, several children ridden down or shot, and a brain-addled teenage boy killed by Pinkertons, working for the railroads. How about the fact that it was Pinks who guarded Abraham Lincoln? 'Nuff said on that one. The great detectives. Yeah . . . in a pig's ass."

Miles lapsed into silence for a moment. Then began with an apology. "Sorry about my outburst. I had family on both sides in the late war. Mr. Pinkerton's Great Detectives made no distinction on their part. Now then, about your embassy to Crazy Horse. I've given what you said a lot of thought. There's plenty of land available south of the Black Hills for another agency to be created. I'll initiate the paper work today on recommending it. Actually, the additional staff intended for holding Crazy Horse and his people on the Red Cloud agency could be simply moved to the new quarters. That way, Crazy Horse will be safe from the jealousy of the Bad Face clan. Do you think he might receive this offer in a positive manner?"

"It's better than anything brought forth so far. When do I start?"

"Now. Right away. I want this wound up quickly so we can be open to whatever might come out of the Nez Percé situation and still have time to look into these killings. Damn it, I don't want to think it, but it could be we've a murderer lurking in the ranks." At once Miles snorted and amended his last remark. "I mean an *active* murderer, not one in hiding. Grudge killings? Gambling debts? You know the sort of thing I mean."

"What about the missing arms?" Eli queried.

Miles pursed his lips, working them in and out a moment in deep thought. "You've a point. At least somewhere to start. Someone has them, has to do something with them. I'll have Quinlan detail a discreet person to look into that aspect. Meanwhile, good luck. I hope to see you, and Crazy Horse, back here soon."

"Where's he located?"

"Last report had him up in the Wind River country."

"You're going to have to make provisions for some of Frank Corrington's good brandy, Colonel."

"Why's that?"

"It never helps on these tough sons of bitches, but it does ease the pain at the start. The Blackfeet have claims to that country and they'll be stalking the camp. I'll be till hell grows icebergs running down Crazy Horse and getting him back here, provided he's willing to come."

Flute song filled the lush, verdant valley. Here and there, on the shaped slopes, patches of snow remained, some deeper than a mounted man's head. A brisk coolness carried on the wind. Despite the heavy love notes, a plaintive sadness filled Hein-mot Too-ya-la-kekt's heart.

It walked with him constantly these days, ever since the time when he'd received word from General Howard that he and his people must be in the Wallowa Valley by April first of the white man's calender. Such a move would be difficult. More than that, nearly impossible.

"Chief Joseph," Howard had appealed, using the name by which whites knew him, "my people and yours will continue to suffer so long as they are pushed too closely together. In the Wallowa Valley, you will have a permanent home, protected by the army and held in perpetuity for your people."

"Is this not what you told us about our traditional grazing and hunting grounds? That we would be safe and protected there, that no whites would come?"

"I—ah, I . . . Yes, I suppose that is what you were promised. Only, you have to understand. . ."

"What I 'understand,' " Joseph had told him, closest he had ever come to open anger against a white soldier leader, "is that your word was broken. Not by you or your soldiers, not by your white

41

governor of Oregon. But by your white brothers, which is to say the same. You wish us to move. We must, by need, conduct our traditional winter elk hunt on our rightful tribal lands. These things are in conflict. Yet, each must be done. The white man takes and the red man dwindles away. We will move as you say. How much time do we have?"

That is when Howard set the time as April 1. It had made the decision even harder for Joseph, and the other sub-chiefs, to keep. In addition to the annual elk hunt, the people now kept cattle for a meat source, along with their herds of the beautiful, spotted-rump Palouse horses. The white man's month of March was the time of birthing. Cows calved, horses foaled. Reflection on these matters only emphasized their complexity and difficulty. The flute music mocked him, rather than soothed.

"You're distracted, Hein-mot Too-ya-la-kekt," Joseph's brother observed as he walked to the large sun-warmed boulder on which the brooding chief sat.

"So would you be. We have few days to accomplish what Howard wants."

"To the Underground with Howard!" Ollokot snapped angrily.

"So far, barring a few incidents, we have lived at peace with the whites. It could be fatal to change all that at this late date. There are more of them," Joseph cautioned, "than we have people, or bullets, or arrows. To move to the Wallowa is but a small thing. We'll do it and, through our friends, appeal to the Great Father in their village called Wash-sing-ton."

"They'll have deaf ears, I warrant you," Ollokot responded prophetically.

"The spring floods have come," Joseph observed to change the subject. "It will make the last part of our journey more difficult."

"Yes. Particularly for you, what with your younger wife great with child. *Why can't we stay in our own lands?*"

"We will be," Joseph soothed. "Only a smaller portion of them. That's all. I must go see Song Bird. She chafes with worry. The Snake is fat and swollen with water. Fording it will be deadly. She must be reassured."

"Rather we made a bridge of white bodies and crossed the river at our leisure," Ollokot snarled to his brother's departing back.

"Aageh . . . Aageh . . . Aageh!" In great whooping discharges, Private Randy Collins expelled the vomit that gagged and burned at his throat. With a final, mighty heave, he emptied his stomach and, still bent over, tried to summon help.

"Cug—Cug—Corporal Ormesby, o-over here," Collins gulped out.

They had been searching in the rotted snowbanks since right after reveille formation. Simmons had been missing. None of his equipment, nor any horses, had likewise taken unauthorized leave of the post. His angry company commander had sent men into the field to search for sign of Simmons. Captain Mason had not bothered to inform K Company of his quite real concern over what they might find.

Corporal Tanner appeared instead, along with Sergeant Pallisier. "What is it, Private Collins?" the senior noncom demanded.

With a limp arm, Collins pointed to a slight rise on the near side of the stand of cottonwoods. "He's over there."

"Frozen?" Tanner asked, then amended his own

suggestion. "No, that couldn't be. It didn't get cold enough last night. What the hell is it, Collins? You look like you've seen a ghost."

"Not a ghost, Corporal," Collins responded, face pale and drawn, eyes staring about wildly. "A c-c-corpse. Simmons's corpse. H-h-heee had his th-throat cu-cu-cu—slit."

"Oh, shit," Sergeant Pallisier exploded. "Another one of them. Tanner, get Lieutenant Hildebrand over here."

"Yeah, Sergeant. Jeez, another croaker. Killed like the others, too, eh?"

"Get moving, you fucking ghoul!" Pallisier barked.

"Th-there's been more?" Collins blurted.

"Where've you been, Collins? This is the fifth one in four weeks. The sergeant major's having a fit over it, Miles is having worse, and if it isn't stopped, the whole army brass will be shitting themselves. Worse, from the way I— Never mind, Collins, show me where you found him," Pallisier cut off abruptly, aware he had revealed too much of himself and the mystery to a common private.

"D-do I have to?"

"You don't have to look."

A minute later, Sergeant William Pallisier wished *he* hadn't looked.

Chapter 5

Fresh shoots of buffalo grass had barely broken the surface of the soil. At least the ground was no longer frozen to a hardness like a rock. All across the wide expanse of Dakota Territory the ice had left the streams, though here and there thin skeins of it extended a few inches out from the banks. Nearly into the Moon of Leaves Returning, such considerations could not deter Bear's Paw and Rabbit Ears from having a swim.

Icy water held no fear for the Oglala boys. Although their band no longer roamed the wide prairie, and home was a place called the Spotted Tail Agency, their way of life had altered little. In winter they would play on the thick ice that covered that same creek, sometimes entirely naked on a sunny day, laughing and shrieking in delight. Now they wasted no time in casting off breechcloths and moccasins and plunging into the frigid waters. Other boys would soon be coming from the camp, but they wanted to be first.

Bear's Paw and Rabbbit Ears had known eleven summers on the prairie, only the last two of them at the reservation. The best of friends, they looked forward to this summer, when they would be granted the privilege of riding on their first hunt. It was all a part of the happy world they found themselves in as they surfaced and yipped shrilly over the cold.

"We are first," Rabbit Ears cried triumphantly.

"No one can take it from us," his friend stated firmly.

"When the others come, they'll find us already in the water," Rabbit Ears continued the story of their childish triumph.

"*Hau!*" Bear's Paw agreed. "If our lips don't turn blue and our toes start to ache."

"Too cold for you?" his companion teased.

A distant sound of hoofbeats sent them into a fit of giggles. Broken Back, a braggart boy of thirteen summers, would burn with envy they knew. He had always been first at everything. Rabbit Ears first recognized the subtle difference a shod hoof made striking the turf. He pointed in the direction from which the sound came.

"That's not . . ."

"Shusssh!" Bear's Paw cautioned.

Soundlessly the Oglala lads slipped from the water and slithered up the low cut-bank, to peer over the top. Faces screened by winter-withered tufts of grass, they looked onto an odd, disturbing scene.

Two white men rode toward them. Behind came the dark, slow-moving forms of cattle. At least five hands of them, Rabbit Ears estimated. The *wasicun* came closer. Less than twenty feet away, the strangers halted.

"Keep on headin' 'em. I'm gonna fill my canteen," Charlie Davis informed the man at his side.

"Don't take too long. We gotta get these critters clear the hell offa the agency before nightfall."

"You can handle 'em, Bluey," Charlie assured his companion. "Gee-up."

Thankful for the slick mud, Rabbit Ears and Bear's Paw slid on their bellies to the water's edge. Their clothes and their ponies waited on the far bank. Swiftly they sank below the surface of the frigid stream and propelled themselves soundlessly toward the opposite shore. Somewhat beyond the midpoint, they came up for a breath. Black-haired heads bobbing in the slight chop, they looked at the white man, who knelt at the water's edge.

"What t'hell. Hey, Bluey, there's been someone down here," Charlie Davis called to Bluey Hanks. "Bluey, you hear me?"

These words meant nothing, but frightened at the sound, the Oglala boys dipped below the surface and streaked for the bank. "What can we do?" Rabbit Ears asked shakily when they came up in a clump of reeds.

"We can get out," Bear's Paw advised him. "The *wasicun* are stealing our cattle."

Rabbit Ears began to shiver. "We can't stay here either. The chiefs have to be told. Warriors have to stop them."

"That white man will kill us if we show ourselves," Bear's Paw whispered back, his voice trembling with cold.

"Look, there's the other one."

"What do you see, Charlie?" Bluey Hanks inquired as he squatted beside his partner.

"Look there. A footprint. Kid most likely. An' there. Another one. We gotta catch 'em before they get away and warn the growed-ups."

"Catch 'em an' what, Charlie?"

"Kill 'em, Bluey."

"Lehman ain't gonna like that."

"We ain't got any choice. We can take their bodies along for a while, dump 'em somewhere else."

Bluey scanned the distant bank. After three careful sweeps, he started, then pointed. "Over there. In them reeds."

"Shit. We can't shoot 'em, it'd attract attention."

"What do we do, Charlie?"

"Go after them," Charlie responded with a grimace of distaste. He sat back and started to remove his boots.

"I'll stay back, case they try to play it smart."

"Good idea. But no guns, Bluey."

Eyes wide, Bear's Paw realized that the men would come after them. "They can't see our ponies. We've got to slip through the grass and get away."

"What about our clothes?"

"Leave them."

By then, Charlie had waded to mid-stream. Wearing only his longjohns and hat, his gunbelt slung over his shoulder, he fought the swift, icy current, water swirling around up to his ribs. From behind he heard Bluey call to him.

"They're outta the water, Charlie. Two little bastards. Crawlin' toward that knob."

"I don't . . . Yeah, I see 'em now." Stealth forgotten, Charlie forged rapidly forward.

He hit the hole, which made this spot a favorite to the Oglala boys, and floudered in over his head. His hat took off for other parts and he made a frightful sound when he surfaced. He swam a few clumsy, inexpert strokes until his feet touched bottom again. Then he surged up out of the creek and shook vigorously. He reoriented himself and started off after the youngsters.

"Run, Rabbit Ears!" Bear's Paw shouted.

Both boys came up with a bound and darted toward their ponies. Roaring with anger, Charlie Davis came after them. From the far bank Bluey's shout urged him on.

"Shoot 'em! Shoot 'em, Charlie."

"I can't! Too much noise."

He gained on the lads, closing to near arm's reach.

Inspiration came and he drew a long-bladed belt knife from its sheath. Thrusting with it, he punctured skin, though did little damage. A thin cry came from the boy, then silence as pursuer and pursued continued to run. Charlie thrust again and drove an inch of steel into Rabbit Ears's bronze back. He stumbled slightly and gritted his teeth. Ahead of him, Bear's Claw swung his wiry body atop his pony. His rein in his teeth, clutching that of Rabbit Ears's mount in one hand, he drummed his bare heels into ribs and bolted toward the advancing pair.

"Hurry," he shouted as he flung the second rein to his friend.

Rabbit Ears made a wild leap that put him clinging sideways against the flank of his pony. With one leg and an arm over the top, he veered away from danger and wriggled to come upright. Cursing foully, Charlie stood helpless and watched the naked youths disappear.

"Goddamnit, Lehman sure ain't gonna like this," he concluded his wrath.

During the time since the last sighting by army scouts, Crazy Horse and his band had moved further south of the Wind River country. His numbers had swollen considerably, Eli Holten discovered when he approached the camp. Many "have not" refugees from other bands had come in, following Miles's successful campaign the previous winter. Quite a few loafers and malcontents had deserted the agencies also.

"They're a great nuisance," Crazy Horse complained to Eli regarding these reservation jumpers, after the formal greetings had been completed. "They have forgotten how to do for themselves and are always complaining."

"Why don't you run them off?" Eli inquired logically.

"They are Oglala. My people. Your people, too, Tall Bear."

"You do look troubled, Crazy Horse. I gather the reason is the number of mouths you have to feed."

"Those who cannot feed themselves, yes. There's more, Tall Bear. Though we have many ponies in our herd, game is scarce. Worse than any time before. I doubt there's enough young buffalo cows to be killed for skins to lodge all the homeless, let alone the lazy and discontent. I, too, have troubles. My woman, Black Shawl, has the lung fever and needs the white man's medicine."

Eli considered a long moment. "Then maybe I come with good news. I speak for the soldier-chief Bear Coat Miles. He knows of the bad blood between you and the Bad Faces, over the Shirt. He has promised to me that he will make arrangements for a new, separate agency for you and your people. You'll not be put close to Red Cloud, Woman's Dress, or the others in the Bad Faces clan. He will also see that the medicine is made available for Sinaspa."

"You're still *tonweya* for the soldier-chief at Rawlins?" At Holten's verification, he went on. "Why do you ride for Bear Coat?"

"Orders from my chief sent me there," Eli answered.

Crazy Horse nodded. "With us it's sometimes the same. Do you believe Bear Coat when he promises this place alone for my people, Tall Bear?"

Eli took longer mulling over this question. "I . . . do. Yes, Crazy Horse, I think you can trust him. I explained about the jealousy of Red Cloud and Woman's Dress when you became a member of the Shirt Wearer society instead of Woman's Dress, whom Red Cloud favored. Also of the bad blood No Water holds against you. He knows he would have more trouble than peace if you were all thrown together on one reservation."

"What do the *wasicun* care?" Crazy Horse asked bitterly. "Not Bear Coat, for he is a warrior and fights by the rules. The others, I ask you, what of them?"

"I could be optimistic and speak words that might not be true. In my heart, I cannot trust them. The politicians speak out of one side of their faces, while their hearts keep secret counsel with the other side."

Crazy Horse snorted, a sound of approval among the Sioux. "You give wise advice. Yet, the hungry and homeless grow every moon and my wife weakens. I will consider what Bear Coat says in this message. Meanwhile, *ta ta iciya wo*. Tonight we'll make a feast and tomorrow you can go back to Bear Coat. I will send a sign to Bear Coat when I have decided."

Relax? Eli Holten wondered. His reception had been cordial enough, yet Crazy Horse was known to be changeable. Complex, like he had told Nelson Miles. The Lakota expression had another, more literal and ominous meaning: *Make yourself as if dead.*

Harlowe Twiss, ex-major of the Union Army, an agent at the Spotted Tail reservation, sat at his desk, turned partway into the room. He ran long, thick fingers through his thinning salt-and-pepper hair and studied the eager faces of the two small boys standing in his office. From a pocket of his elk-hide hunting shirt he removed a pair of thick-lensed spectacles, wiped at the smudges on the glass with a bandanna, and placed them on his long, Roman nose.

"Now, then, go through that again," he requested in precise Lakota.

Bear's Paw and Rabbit Ears, once more in breechcloths, moccasins, and lightweight shirts, rolled rounded eyes. They drew deep breaths and began their tale again. They spoke alternately, small hands making short, sharp gestures to emphasize their points.

"We were first at the swimming place," Bear's Paw declared.

"First in the water," Rabbit Ears added.

"Rabbit Ears heard some horses coming. I thought it was our friends. Oh, how they would be full of envy at our being first. So . . ."

"When the horses came closer, Bear's Paw said they sounded like *wasicun* horses. So we went to take a . . ."

Bit by bit the story unfolded. At the conclusion, when it came to Rabbit Ears's wound, he turned around and raised his shirt to expose a bandage and poultice prepared by the medicine healer. When he did, he saw the glittering, admiring eyes of the Twiss youngsters. Eight pair of obsidian orbs fixed on him, from eight bronze, half-Brule faces. The older two boys had been with those who had intercepted him and Bear Paw on the way back from the creek.

"*Hecitu yele*," Bear Paw insisted sternly. "That's true," he repeated. "They took our cows. They tried to kill Rabbit Ears and me."

"I, ah, see." Major Twiss leaned back in the rickety chair to contemplate.

He didn't use this office often, preferring to live among his charges, as one of them, with his still-attractive Brule wife and eleven children. Harlowe

Twiss had little use for the army. His opinion had altered greatly when he'd observed the bloodthirsty, often venal, excesses of Sherman's butchers, during the campaign through Georgia to the sea at Charleston, South Carolina. Disillusioned and embittered, Twiss mustered out at the end of hostilities and ventured west. He met and came to love the woman who became his wife. She in turn had taught him the language and delivered him a large brood of half-Sioux offspring. Truth to tell, Harlowe Twiss loved every one of them dearly.

Enough so to trouble him greatly now. Two children, friends of his sons, savagely attacked. Agency beef rustled by unknown whites, not only this once, but from accounts, the herd had been raided regularly. Signs found in profusion on other occasions indicated the culprits might be hostiles. White men added a new dimension. Or had his people become the victims of more than one band of predators? To darken his picture, more unrest had come to his attention that might involve his charges at any time.

Another soldier had been found at Fort Thompson, his throat cut and his weapons gone. The seventh, he'd heard, in six weeks. Small wonder he had no soothing answer for these small boys. He cleared his throat and addressed them gravely.

"I will make a complete report, in which you will both receive mention for your brave actions. In it I'll ask for help. Now that we are alerted to this new danger, something can be done about it. You are both to be admired. Now go on and greet your friends. They'll want to hear all about your adventure."

Chapter 6

Giant black anvils built on the southwestern horizon. Swelling rapidly, they expanded to fill half the sky. Sensitive to the changes in pressure, temperature, and the mysterious charges of the ozone, small animals and birds sought shelter from the impending storm. Flies swarmed around windows and doorways at Fort Thompson. Eli Holten, tired and recently returned from his mission to Crazy Horse, used his wide-brimmed hat to shoo away a thick cluster at the entrance to the headquarters building.

"Welcome back, Mr. Holten," RSM Quinlan greeted cheerily. "Himself'll see ye at once. Go on in."

"Thanks, Quinlan. I've had one hell of a trip."

"Ye'll be findin' we've our own crosses to bear while ye've been gone, I warrant."

"Such as?" Eli asked in hopes of some insight into Miles's mood.

"T'gen'ral will be for tellin' ye, I'm sure."

Stymied from the outset, Eli knocked and entered. Miles offered him a seat and he related his encounter with the Oglala chief. At the conclusion, Miles studied the scout over his steepled fingers.

"Your opinion, Mr. Holten?"

Eli started to answer, then held back, eyes glazing

54

into a far-off look. "Given three things," he said at last, "Crazy Horse will come in."

Mile considered it a moment and made prompt response. "Yes, I agree. Help for his woman, of course, and a separate agency so's not to rub raw the sores on Red Cloud's back, eh? What's the third?"

"A place for the 'have nothings,' as he calls them. The refugees. And with that, the implication is clear for food enough to feed them all."

"Harrrumph! You would bring that up. Have some of that Tennessee mash."

"You have some problem with food?" Eli inquired.

"More than a little. I received this memo from Harlowe Twiss at the Spotted Tail agency. There seems to be some rustling going on. Agency beef being taken away. There have been five recent indications of cattle theft. In the earlier ones, evidence found on the ground points toward hostiles, or perhaps persons from another agency. In particular Twiss suspects warriors from the Red Cloud agency. Since Twiss doesn't get along with George Crook, he's made an appeal to me to do something about it."

"And what's different about this last theft?" Eli caught it up. "Why the distinction?"

"Because this last time there were witnesses. Two small boys out for a swim saw white men driving agency cattle."

"Could they have been delivering them?" Eli questioned.

"Possible. Twiss says none were due at that particular time. Yet it could have been someone hoping to get a jump on the spring rains. I'm not a cowman . . ."

"Nor am I," Eli inserted in Miles's remarks.

". . . so I'm in need of someone to serve as my eyes and ears inside the agencies, to determine if stock is

55

also being stolen from them, also to develop any connection. I don't know cows, but I do know Indians, and so do you. To the Sioux, raids to steal horses, women, or children are considered sort of like a game played against fierce rivals. It's entirely possible that you might dig out something to substantiate this. Or get a lead on any white men who might be involved. Meanwhile I intend to keep the pressure on Crazy Horse, let him know we insist on his coming in."

"A tall order on both counts, Colonel," Eli observed. "How's the situation with the Nez Percé going?"

"Fairly well. Chief Joseph complied with General Howard's deadline in good order. He and his people are in the Wallowa Valley. Hopefully that'll be the end of it."

"So then, we sit and wait for Crazy Horse?" Eli asked lightly.

"There's a bit more, I'm afraid. My command has had eight men murdered in a bit less than nine weeks. We discussed it earlier, as I'm sure you recall. I'm loath even now to call in the Pinkertons. What I need is someone who can move around freely and unobtrusively and get some sort of handle on this. So, I'm afraid I'll want you to do somewhat more than sit," Miles returned.

Eli raised a large hand in protest. "I'm no more a detective than I am a cowman. What I know's Indians."

"I'm aware of that and, in both instances, there's indication enough that Indians might be involved. I'll make my earlier suggestion an order if I need to . . ." He let it hang.

"No need, Colonel," Eli replied with a groan of resignation. "Only, when you get a tough one for me,

I'd appreciate it if you'd check with Frank Corrington first."

"Through channels, eh?"

"No. I had in mind you finding out his brand of cigars and the label on that good brandy of his. He always has them around to mollify me when I get the smelly, brown end of the stick."

Laughing, the scout excused himself and left the office.

Sweet William, her off-wheeler, had been acting up all morning. Obstinate, as only a mule can be, he had kicked at the traces, bellowed his discontent for all the world to hear, and shirked his share of the load as much as could be done in a six-up on a big Conestoga freighter. Small wonder Jenny Blanchard considered herself ready to skin him for mule meat by the time she reached Fort Thompson.

Cursing the animal malevolently, she brought her rig to a stop at the quartermaster warehouse. She climbed off the lazy board and set the brake, while muttering another imprecation against the mule's ancestory. Sweet William swung his head around and attempted to take a nip from her shoulder. Jenny rapped Sweet William on the nose with the lead-loaded haft of her whip.

"I'm going to trade you for a Clydesdale," she threatened. Then her personality underwent a radiant change when a voice spoke behind her.

"I missed you," Eli Holten declared in a quiet, firm tone.

Jenny whirled and embraced him. "Eli!"

The round knocker pommel on her whip rapped him lightly behind one ear. She squeezed tightly and raised her legs off the ground, so that he held her in his big arms, pressed against his chest. Her lips missed their mark slightly and caught him on the corner of his mouth. It made his voice come out oddly when he spoke through their embrace.

"You either rapped me a good one with that whip handle, or I think I'm in love."

"Lout!" she exclaimed as she broke the kiss. "Churl! Beast! Is that any way to greet a lady?"

"Not exactly," Eli answered lightly. "But then, dressed like that, who's to know you're a lady?"

"Ooooh! You wait. I'll get you for that. If—if there was a water trough around here I'd push you into it."

"Hey, take it easy now. Let me help you unload and then we can go get something to eat. There's a Chinaman whose opened a really good dinner hall. Some strange kinds of food, right enough, but good tasting. There's a thing he calls 'won ton soup' "—Eli pronounced it *wanton*—"with little meat pies in it. And something called 'got let chicken.' And little-bitty spareribs . . ."

"Is eating all you can think about?" Jenny asked coyly.

Eli's grin spread clear across his face. "Well, there *is* a little something else I had in mind."

"We'll have days and days of it, don't you worry," Jenny said dreamily as she began unfastening the rope that lashed down the canvas cover of her wagon.

Holten's frown sobered them both. "There won't be much time for that. You're getting here and I'm leaving. At least I will be tomorrow."

"Why? Why so soon?"

"Colonel Miles. He wants me to look into these murders of soldiers, and some cattle stealing going on up at the Spotted Tail agency."

"That's work for a scout?" Jenny asked dubiously.

"I tried to convince him of that, only he wasn't listening. At least we have the rest of today."

"And tonight. All of tonight."

To her pleasure, Jenny found the meal to be as delicious as Eli had pictured it. They drank tea from small glazed clay cups and stared deeply into each other's eyes. Jenny grew expansive when talk turned to her business.

"I'm going to get another in. A big tandem Conestoga. I've already got the reserve draft animals. What I need is a swamper."

"Is that a job offer?" Eli asked lightly.

Jenny wrinkled her nose. "No, silly. I need a strong, healthy boy, to help with the harnessing, care for the mules and such, do scut work around camp at in-between stops. An apprentice, so's to speak. Thing is, what I want is someone young enough not to be gettin' randy and trying to put his charms on his boss."

"Hummmm," Eli mused, a vague image forming in his mind. "How young is what you call young?"

"Oh, twelve, thirteen or so," Jenny answered.

"If he was real strong, stocky built, say, could he be a little younger?"

Jenny's eyes sparkled. "You've got someone in mind? Is that it? Sure, he could be a year or so younger . . . if he was mighty strong."

"How about a husky kid raised on a homestead, who survived a Sioux raid last Christmas, then rode and walked a hundred miles to where they're building Fort Keogh to report it?"

"My God. I'd take him in a hot tic."

"One thing, though. He doesn't speak a word of English. He's a German boy."

Concentration wrinkled Jenny's brow. "He probably wouldn't know the names of everything on a freighter anyway. So he can learn his English while he learns that. Is he a hard worker?"

"I think so. He went right to it at Keogh. A carpenter and his wife took him in temporarily.

"Will he still be there? I've got a load of nails, hinges, and other hardware for there in three days. I could get a look."

"Last I heard he hadn't moved on. His name's Martin Richter, and he was ten years old last Christmas."

"Ten? He lived through all that? Yeah, Eli, I think he'd make a great swamper."

Half an hour later, Jenny nuzzled her cheek into the hollow of Eli's bare shoulder. They lay in her bed, partially satiated from a hurried first coupling. Jenny slowly rubbed her leg along the inside of Eli's left thigh. The tingly contact stirred new life in his long, lax member.

"Why do I feel so downright *good* when I'm with you, like this?" Jenny murmured.

"I don't know," Eli responded drowsily.

"I'm so warm and comfortable, so . . . safe."

"By golly, Jenny, I didn't know I was a father figure."

"Rat!" she squeaked.

Instantly she clamped a hand on his proud lance and swiftly worked it to rigid attention. She breathed rapidly and harshly as she slathered her tongue over the blunt tip. Slowly she took him in. One hand kneaded the soft pouch at the base of his staff, while the other inscribed circles on his belly. She swallowed roughly and ingested more of his burning flesh. A wild thrill coursed through her as Eli lifted her hips and swung her into line atop his chest. Sheer ecstacy exploded in her groin as he speared his tongue deep

60

within her tingling cleft.

In a riot of rapt delight they lapped and gulped and strained to give and receive the utmost. Jenny could feel Eli's heart pound against her belly and her own galloped out of control in response. She returned a hand to the ample length of his phallus that remained outside her lips. Feather-light, she stroked and teased the silken pole. Another prodigious swallow put her over the barrier.

Speedily she let his manhood slide on down until her lips nuzzled in the thick thatch of his pubic hair. She had him all. Every bit. Galvanized by her sensual accomplishment, Eli arched his back and began to pump his hips. Jenny began to hum. In moments the lights whirled and a chorus of angels sang for Eli as he erupted into liquid oblivion, while jolt after jolt of incredibly wild sensation seared through his nerves.

"Now *that*," Jenny assured him once she had withdrawn his magnitude from deep in her throat, "is something I'd never dream of giving my father, a figurative one or not. Are you happy?"

"I'm ruined, destroyed. You nearly pulled it out by the roots."

Jenny released a tinkling peal of laughter. "I've something better qualified for that job, as you're soon to see," she promised coyly. "Want to give it a try?"

"Right now I'm too played out for anything."

"Oh, no, you're not," Jenny declared as she bent his still-rigid shaft downward and released it so that it popped back in place.

In a wild scramble, she arranged herself on hands and knees. "Come on, my fine stallion," she urged with a glance over her shoulder at Eli. "You've got a mare in terrible need."

Rousing to the game, Eli positioned himself behind her, kneeling on the creaky bed. Slowly he slid the upper surface of his penis between her legs until the questing tip encountered the hot lips of her moist and welcoming portal. Dainty pink petals parted to receive his languorous thrust, which cleaved her entryway and gained him access to Cupid's channel beyond.

"Aaaayyyyiii!" Jenny squealed. "Oh, yes. Now, now, now. More, Eli, more."

He grasped her slender hips with both big hands and delivered an additional length. Jenny began to tremble. With a determined slam of his hips he hilted himself in her silken garden. Jenny moaned and thrashed her head. Masterful in his control, Eli churned his stiffened lance within a foamy sea of warmth and slithery friction.

All thought of duty and danger departed from him as he sent powerful waves of erotic scintillation through them both. It would be, he knew, a long and unbelievably wonderful night.

Chapter 7

Ecstacy also swam in the mind of a young trooper assigned to General George Crook's command. Detailed to police the Red Cloud agency, it was understandable why Lance Williams was so excited over the prospect of wetting his wick in a ready and willing woman. Half an hour after he'd come off duty, Lance had washed, shaved, and splashed bay rum on his raw jaw. Dressed in his best, mindful of regulations about not going about unarmed, he departed the cantonment area in search of his passionate beauty.

He found her at the appointed place. They wasted few words as each hurriedly removed sufficient clothing to accomplish the purpose of their encounter. Rigid and reddened, his unremarkable penis responded almost unbearably to the lightest touch. Lordy how long, long overdue this was, Lance reflected as the sweet-faced, lithe woman ran light fingers over his manhood, sending shivers of sheer delight through his body.

It made him want to shriek and squeal, like he had the first time he came. Lordy, after ten long months assigned among this swarm of heathens, he must have flogged his mule more times than in all the years when he was a kid. Nothing for it, though, except some fat, ugly squaws who hung out around the agency headquarters and would screw for a bottle of cheap whiskey. Ugh! Well, ol' Lance had found a far better choice. He reached out and took her in his arms. They sank to the ground, on a blanket he had brought.

Shaking like a scared kid on his first time, Lance thrust himself inside her hot, moist cavity. Long abstinence became his undoing, as he began to thrust and rock wildly in a frenzy of suppressed lust. Long before he wanted it, he felt the sensation rising from his groin, tightening his belly and bursting in colored stars in his mind. And, oh . . . oh . . . ooooh! How good it felt as he let go.

A moment later another sensation burned within Lance Williams's body. Huge and razor-sharp, the butcher knife was driven under his skin, through the corded muscle and into his right kidney. Choking on incredible pain, paralized into helplessness and unable to make a sound, blackness became Lance's final orgasm.

His fears had not been unfounded, Chief Joseph reflected sadly as he sat in the sun in front of his lodge in the Wallowa Valley. The Snake River crossing had been a disaster. In his mind he still heard the shrill cries of young horses, of women and children. The churning waters had come on them, an evil gray-brown color, rolling, froth-topped. Huge foamy platforms of white spume dashed against rocks and whisked away. Men and animals had disappeared in the tumult, some of them showing up again, dripping, on the far shore. Many had not.

Nearly all of the herd's increase had been lost, the tally showed later. Along with several old people, a healthy young woman and one child. It made his heart heavy with grieving. Careful to keep his face blank, Joseph, whose tribal name translated as Thunder Traveling to Loftier Heights, leaned back in his woven-reed backrest and confronted the angry face of his brother.

"Too-hool-hool-zote wants to fight the white men. To drive them from our lands. I am of the same mind."

Behind Ollokot, the keening of the women could be heard still mourning the dead. Hein-mot Too-ya-la-kekt nodded toward it, as though it were a tangible entity. Slowly he spoke his thoughts.

"Our losses are tragic, not the least our traditional lands. Yet, the grieving of our women is tempered somewhat for me by the certain knowledge that I have averted a war our people can't win."

"Howard's men are few," Ollokot insisted stubbornly.

"Over the talking wire, Howard can summon more soldiers than there are entirely among the *Nimpau*; men, women, and even children. We are not so many as to be foolish enough to waste our lives on the soldiers' knives."

"It's not a waste! Can't you see that, Hein-mot?"

"I cannot. Neither can you, if you'd let reason rule your tongue."

"You will do nothing, then? What if Howard comes again, saying we must move on to yet another place?"

"Then we shall move."

"And when he asks what you cannot give?"

"I am not so empty-headed as to not prepare for such an eventuality. That is why I depleted our precious horse herd even more to purchase arms and ammunition from that Cayuse chief before we en-

65

tered this country. Now, leave me with this talk of war. I must think of what we will do next."

Another rain was building up. Even without a cloud in the sky, he could smell it. Duncan McAllister sat in a small, cramped room of his main ranch house. Lighted only by the sunny spill through a tall, narrow window with damask curtains and heavy drapes, the library, as McAllister laughingly called it, had a gloomy atmosphere, despite the bright motes struck by the outdoor light. Through the open lower portion of the window came the soft lowing of cattle in their pens, as they shifted about and reacted to unseen warnings of an impending change in weather, much like their owner. Across a small table from McAllister, which held a chess board, a crystal decanter, and two glasses, sat Walter Lehman. Lehman had just hesitantly placed his queen's knight at McAllister's queen's three, threatening the rancher's queen's bishop and placing the king in check.

"Check, Duncan."

"Ummmm," McAllister mulled the problem. "Now then, we're doing rather well, as I'm sure you know, Walter."

Lehman exhibited a broad smile. "So long as I'm providing you with cattle and you're providing me with money, we haven't a worry in the world."

"I'm far from being frivolous about all this. It's unfortunate that your men encountered those Indian boys. By now, every savage from the Mississippi to Yellowstone will know about it. It will make your work more difficult. And right at a time when I was prepared to offer you a full partnership."

"A part— Ah, Duncan, I'm surprised."

McAllister chuckled. "I rather thought you'd be.

66

I've obtained title and lease rights to more land. The ranch is a lucrative enterprise. I need to expand. And . . . ah . . ." he drew out as he swooped onto the board and slashed Lehman's knight out of play with a heretofore hidden bishop. "Guard your queen."

"I'll be damned. I never thought . . ."

"Chess is a game for devious minds. In the future, see that your men exercise a little more deviousness. Twenty-five head aren't enough profit to risk this entire operation for. They should have shot those boys, broken up their gather, and gotten out of there. But that's all history, like your rather crude knight-queen gambit that failed. While you devise some means to extricate yourself from my threat to your queen, let's consider the future."

Lehman directed his attention to the board while McAllister poured more brandy for both of them. If he stayed where he was, he would lose his queen. If he withdrew, it would give McAllister time to deploy an attack of his own. If he charged in and hoped for the best, he'd also lose his queen.

"I'm delighted by talk that Crazy Horse might be coming in. When you first brought word of it to me I began efforts to obtain more pasture. There'll be at least another five hundred to a thousand head a year to pick and choose from if the last of the hostiles are put on reservation. The advantage to our growing empire is obvious. Crazy Horse and his band represent a fine new source for increasing the fortunes of the Box M. Well, partner, what do you say?" McAllister concluded, lifting his snifter in a toast.

"To more and bigger profits," Walter Lehman responded.

"Amen to that," Duncan McAllister said as Lehman moved his queen. "And . . . knight takes knight, check. Mate in a move." His laughter bounced from the high paneled walls.

Short hauls, Jenny Blanchard reasoned, would keep her around Fort Thompson often enough so that she and Eli could keep up their romantic involvement. So far her scheming hadn't accomplished its purpose, and it did leave her with rather unpleasant cargoes of mixed lots. Like the one she carried at the present time.

Kegs of gunpowder, coarse-grained stuff for the cannons, and touchy to deal with. Also men's pants. Crate after crate of black trousers. She had picked up the mismatched commodities at Fort Randall, where they had been offloaded from a steamboat. The hundred-mile return trip had been accomplished in twelve miserable days. Plagued by spring rains, impossible ruts, and belligerent boulders, Jenny had all but despaired of completing the journey. One bright spot had lightened her burden.

She had taken her military consignment to Fort Keogh and met young Martin Richter. A German-speaking sergeant had made her offer clear to the boy and he had wept with happiness at the prospect. Without delay he had gathered up his few belongings and scrambled into the wagon. The sturdy, stocky lad had earned his keep twenty times over since then. Particularly when they'd been mired hub-deep in the mud on the way back from Randall. Along the way, his already-acquired partial command of English improved remarkably.

He could say "Oh, hell," "Damned rain," and "Son of a bitch!" without any sign of an accent. Martin's dark eyes and solemn expression often provided a stimulus to Jenny's flagging sense of humor. His most despairing look could bring forth peals of

68

musical laughter. He rode the spring seat of the emigrant-rigged Conestoga without complaint and often exercised his growing vocabulary with descriptions of the wonders of the land around them. Jenny wanted to hug him and pet him and hold him close in the night, though she refrained from doing so. After all, she was his boss, not his mother. They sat side by side, chatting about the habits of the prairie grouse, when the wagon rolled to a stop outside the quartermaster warehouse at Fort Thompson.

"What? Not blasted to smithereens?" the QM sergeant inquired sarcastically when Jenny stepped down.

"No thanks to you, Flannery. You have some men to give me a hand?"

"Alas, no. That I don't. You an' the lad'll be havin' to do it for yerselves."

"Damn it, Flannery, I think you delight in makin' it tough on me."

"Me? Why, saints preserve, I'd never do a thing like that. Happens all me hearties are out on monthly rifle drill. Shootin' at far marks they are. So, best be getting about it."

"Marty," she spoke to the boy. "We've got to unload ourselves."

"Oh, shit," Martin responded in perfect imitation of her tone when using the expletive.

Barely tall enough to see over the high side of the wagon, Martin had to teeter the crates over the side and release them to be caught by Jenny. One such he let go, only to have it strike her hand wrong and crash to the ground. The splintering noise attracted Sergeant Flannery.

"Here now, what's all this. That's government prop'ity yer mishandlin'."

Then he stopped to stare, mystified like Jenny, at

the contents. "That's not *Men's Trousers, Regimental Band Black, Assorted Sizes*," Flannery said wonderingly. "It's nothin' but moldy prairie hay. What have ye to say for yerself about that, Miss Jenny Blanchard?"

"I—I've nothing to say, because I don't know anything more about it than you do."

"A fine story that is. Ye've no doubt been sneakin' off a bit o' this and that over a long time now, to sell on the outside at a big profit, eh? I've caught ye redhanded now an' it's the quartermaster himself ye'll be answerin' to."

Flannery reached out and grabbed at Jenny's wrist. A dark-haired, freckle-faced fury leaped upon his shoulders then. It gave a banshee wail and began to pound his bare head.

"Leef her *frei*, son of a bitch!" Martin cried out.

For all that he had yet to see eleven, the stout ex-farm boy packed a wallop. Flannery had his ears ring and spots dance before his eyes before he managed to fix thumb and forefinger on one of Martin's ears and give a good twist.

"*Gott in Himmel, das ist schwer!* Damn you to hell!" he bellowed in his oddly mixed language usage.

With a twist of his arm, Flannery yanked Martin free of his shoulders. "Ye'll be goin' in to face charges of theft, too, ye foul whelp."

"Let him go or I'll take your hide off with this whip," Jenny warned coldly. Eyes ablaze, she shook out her road leather and menaced the vengeance-hungry NCO.

"Ye'll be rottin' in prison before ye do that," Flannery defied her, giving Martin's ear a vicious turn.

Whiteness appeared around Jenny's lips and she started her arm back. Suddenly a big hand grasped

70

her right biceps and arrested her motion.

"Jenny, Jenny, what's brought all this on?" Eli Holten inquired in a humorously chiding tone.

"Oh, Eli. He—he accused me, us, of stealing some damned old pants. Black uniform trousers."

"Why the whip? Why not simply go in, tell Major Grimes your story, and be done with it?"

"Look! Look what he's doing to Martin."

Eli obeyed and his light, far-seeing gray eyes turned to slate. "Let him go, Sergeant, or I'll gleefully break your fingers, one—at—a—time."

"Ye've got a big mouth, bucko."

"My fist is even bigger."

"Aaah, the devil take ye all." With ill grace, Flannery released Martin and bent to retrieve his kepi. He fitted it on his head, adjusted his tunic, and stalked off with a malevolent backward glance.

"I still oughta hide that son of a bitch," Jenny complained.

"He was only doing his job. It looks like you got taken here. Since I'm already playing detective for Nelson Miles, I'll look into it, if you want."

"Oh, I do want, Eli. So long as you let me come along with you."

The sparkle that began to glow in her eyes had not been forged by anger.

"I think we can arrange something," Eli assured her, his own sparkle rising in his groin.

Chapter 8

Mighty eagles and their lesser cousins, the hawks, in many varieties, made lazy figure-eights, chandelles, and circles in the sky, searching for prey. An aroma of fresh, green newness filled the air. The road between Forts Thompson and Randall had turned to iron-hard ruts. Jenny Blanchard's wagon jolted along with her on the spring seat, while Eli Holten rode alongside on his big Morgan, Sonny. Young Martin Richter remained behind, at Randall, sulking over missing out on the trip. With the cargo box empty, they made better than thirty miles a day. Partway through the third day, Eli decided on a course of action.

"I'm going to ride on ahead and look around. They'll not be expecting you back so soon. Once I've got a feel of the people you named, I'll be able to gauge their reaction when you show up. That should give us an idea of who all is involved."

"I'll miss you tonight," Jenny responded.

Through a grin, Eli agreed. "And I, you. Once this is cleared up, we'll have a little time."

"I certainly hope so."

"Count on it. Now, hold back a bit on this rig. Give me, oh, at least two days. Then come on in."

As quartermaster sergeants go, Michael Marchetti turned out to be better than most and not quite as efficient as some. He kept a separate record of transshipments, as opposed to issue equipment. Eli Holten learned most of this during a discreet conversation with the post commander, Lt. Colonel Bryce Hutton. Hutton felt he had himself a prize gem in the former merchandise-control manager of a warehousing operation in New York City. Eli brought an unwelcome mood of sudden distrust when he patiently explained about the prairie hay.

"Even a hundred miles makes a difference in this climate," the scout observed. "The wildflowers are just budding at Thompson. Here, as I recall, they were in bloom two weeks ago. The hay in that crate had small wildflower blossoms in it. The switch couldn't have been done before shipment from Jefferson Barracks, or the hay would have been completely rotted. It was damp and relatively fresh."

"I don't like it."

"Neither does Miss Blanchard or the quartermaster at Fort Thompson," Eli returned. "Think about it, Colonel. Someone has to have a source to dispose of the sort of item being taken. Who, besides Marchetti, would have such contacts?"

"He's been so . . . efficient," Lieutenant Colonel Hutton stated regretfully.

"There's no proof he is the one," Eli reminded him. "All I ask for is an opportunity to observe without being conspicuous."

"That can be arranged. And be assured this will be kept strictly between you and I. Colonel Miles is putting you to unusual use for a scout, Mr. Holten, but his temper can be formidable and I'm more than willing to cooperate."

For a day, Eli lounged around the fort, observing the routine activities of the four men, including Sergeant Marchetti, who worked in the quartermaster warehouse. That evening, with the connivance of Lieutenant Colonel Hutton, Eli slipped unnoticed into the warehouse. He took along a couple of blankets and arranged a comfortable lair for himself. He might spend the night for nothing.

"What at night?" Hutton had asked.

"During the day everything that moves in or out is seen by too many people. Any shady business has to be conducted in secret," Eli explained.

So he waited, fruitlessly, through the night. The next day, Jenny arrived. Her presence brought no marked change nor strong reaction from Sgt. Michael Marchetti. One of his clerks seemed a bit flustered, and Holten put it down to the fact she was alone and the corporal involved had been known to have tried to make time with her in the past. Her visit proved to be timely in that a small shipment had been made up for an outpost under the authority of Fort Randall. She could haul that, and some supplies the sutler had to send to his brother, who operated the store at Ft. Thompson. Eli would again spend the night in the drafty warehouse.

He entered an hour before Lights Out. Quietly he arranged his observation post and settled in. Thirty minutes later he heard low voices from the vicinity of the rear entrance to the building. His keen hearing straining, Eli made out the words.

"What are you doing here this late?" a young voice demanded.

"Look, I got behind a little, see? Some things that

have to be crated up for that shipment to outpost number three. Miss Jenny's leaving in the morning, so I'd better do it now, or my ass'll be in a sling. It won't take long and nobody will ever know. Let me in and go about your duty. I'll make it worth your while."

"Like what?" the sentry queried. "I could get in a lot of trouble."

"No, you can't. I outrank you, right? This is official quartermaster business, so let me in and I'll show my gratitude with a bottle from the NCO supply at the sutler's."

"I could be in a fix," came the wary response.

"Captain Mannering said I should do it. Look, he even gave me a pass to be out after Taps."

"All right, then," the guard relented a moment later. "You've got the keys?"

"Right here."

A padlock and chain rattled and the door opened with a slight creak. The intruder worked his way between several racks of clothing and field equipment, to a large table with a wooden crate resting on it. He lit a sheltered lamp and examined the contents. Quickly he removed them into a trash can, shiny new pairs of field glasses, and covered the pile with excelsior from a large container under the counter. From another waste bin, which had obviously been brought in earlier, he extracted some fist-sized rocks, which he placed in the original crate. That done, he was preparing to put on the lid when Eli Holten made his move.

Loud as rockfalls in a cave, the hammer of Holten's big Remington .44 ratcheted back to full-cock. He rose in a stooped position under the rafters and centered his six-gun muzzle on the clever thief.

"Hold 'er right there, Corporal," Eli growled.

"Wha—!" Startled, Corporal Peter Carlson, Jenny's would-be suiter, blurted the sound as he looked up.

Quick and resourceful, he snatched a pair of field glasses from the case and hurled them in Eli's direction. Unable to evade the flying object in the cramped space near the roof, Eli took the impact in his chest. That put his aim off, and when his Remington roared, the slug smacked the wall two inches from Carlson's head.

Instantly the dishonest soldier bolted for the door. Holten leaped down on top of him. Carlson gave a loud, explosive grunt as he floundered on the floor. Overbalanced, Eli Holten stumbled past him and turned to find himself facing the naked blade of a saber. Peter Carlson lunged as the scout eared back the hammer of his revolver.

Sharp steel pierced the thin, pliable elkhide of Eli Holten's shirt and pricked the flesh below before his slug slammed into Peter Carlson's chest and propelled him backward. Holten fired again and the saber clattered to the floor. Behind him the door flew open and the sentry stormed in, Springfield at the ready.

"Hold it right there."

"I'm not moving, soldier," Eli answered. "Call the sergeant of the guard and have him send for Colonel Hutton. I've just caught our supply thief."

Confused, the sentry looked from one man to the other. A gurgling, raspy sound came from Carlson's throat. Feebly he raised one hand and waved it in a gesture of dismissal.

"I-I'm not . . . in this . . . alone, H-Holten. Y-you won't last . . . a month. Your blood's guh-guh-gonna be splashed . . . all over the . . . prairie."

"Somehow I don't think I'm going to lose any sleep

over that," Eli coldly told the dying man.

Reins in hand, slumped back until his shoulders touched the backrest of the wagon seat, Eli Holten drove while Jenny Blanchard fumbled with the deer-horn buttons of his fly. Eagerly she drew out his achingly erect organ and began to knead it.

"Now you know why I insisted on Marty staying behind," she told him impishly.

"Why? Afraid you might have to take care of him, too?"

Bent low over the object of her fascination, Jenny bolted upright. "That's sick, Eli. He's just a little boy."

"I know another 'little boy' his age who, according to his family, has been 'foolin' around for a good three years,'" Eli responded, thinking of the Thornes. "You've seen the way Martin looks at you? In a couple more years, you're going to have a raging stallion on your hands."

"When that time comes, I'll take care of it the best way I know how," Jenny answered primly.

Eli produced a broad grin. "The *best way* you know how is exactly what he'll have in mind."

"Eli! How can you live with yourself? You've got such a dirty mind."

"I'm not so old I don't remember what it's like being a youngster," Eli defended. "I know it's popular to think so, and all the churches certainly accept it as positive, that children don't have any sexual inclinations. That's a myth, an old wives' tale. Think about your own childhood. I know that at Martin's age, I knew all about what went on between men and women. I'd probably been lopin' my mule at least for a couple of years."

Jenny made a face, realizing the conversation had gone from the serious to the ridiculous. "You were just a horny little devil, that's all."

"I can't deny that. But my point is, nearly all kids are. Some may hide it, but it's there all the same, pestering them. Most invent, or find out, some means of releasing the pressure. One way or the other, life goes on quite normally, with barely a ripple. When you first brought up getting a swamper, you said that you didn't want one old enough to start making swings at his boss. That implied a knowledge that maybe even you didn't want to discuss.

"Right now you want to mother Martin. I see it clearly every time you're together. If so, do it now, don't hesitate or question your motives. Just do it. Hug him and kiss his cheek and do all those motherly things. Then start building a bit of distance between the two of you. Otherwise, nature will have its way and you'll find yourself haunted by guilt and shame for the rest of your life."

"I, ah . . . Thank you, Eli. I suppose I needed that lecture. I owe you a great deal."

"Such as how much?"

"How about this much?" Jenny replied as she bent low and took Eli's maleness deep within her mouth.

"Ummmm. I'll have to study on this for a while," the scout responded.

Dawn had come clear and bright. This made the day even more radiant. Feathery lips slid over his hot, silken flesh. Shivers of delight coursed through him. Jenny began to do wonderful things with her tongue. Eli stifled a grunt and slumped lower. With one hand he reached inside her paisley shirt and began to gently squeeze her left breast. A haze of contentment settled over the armorous pair. The mules clopped on, oblivious to the ardor of mere humans. Sonny

78

whickered from his place behind the wagon and gave a snort of what might have been disgust. Eli sighed deeply.

"That's good. Oh, that's great," he murmured.

Jenny worked on. Vaguely, Eli noted a clump of cottonwoods on the horizon. If this didn't conclude before they got there, he bargained with himself, he'd stop and they could have a midday romp. Industriously, Jenny ingested more of his throbbing shaft. Eli's belly tensed and the urge to make powerful thrusts burned within his raging loins. When the cottonwood trees stood off the right side of the wagon, Jenny had skillfully managed to hold off his plunge into ecstacy.

Carefully Eli guided the team off the road and into the trees. A crescendo of bright lights momentarily drained the scout as he halted the team. Jenny came up for breath.

"Here? On top of the cargo?" she asked, panting.

"Get some blankets," Eli instructed.

By the time she had arranged their trysting place, Eli had removed his clothes. He took hers off with kisses and skilled fingers. Then, still standing, he lifted Jenny's slight weight and impaled her on his powerful phallus.

"Yeeeeeiiii!" she thrilled as she slid down the length of his bounty. "Let me," Jenny panted, "find something to brace against."

"You've, ah, made love like this before?"

"Only once. With my shy musician. We were in the music room at school, the cloak room. All of a sudden we both had this terrible urge to do it. I pulled up my skirt and took down my bloomers and straddled his hips. With my back braced against the wall we went at it standing up. I thought I'd go crazy. It was so wild, and scary and exciting. Afterward we got cleaned up and straightened around and went out and played Mozart together for a parents' meeting."

"I rest my case."

"What?"

"We were talking earlier about children? You just made my strongest argument for me."

"You louse. If I didn't love you so much, I'd hate you."

"We'd better get busy in the loving department," Eli suggested to her.

"You know, Eli, I've been giving it some consideration."

"About Martin?"

"No. About the killer of these soldiers."

"How'd that come up?" Eli asked testily, his ardor aroused and painfully obvious in his tender, swollen scrotum.

"Association. They'd all been out to, ah, engage in similar, ah, activity, right? So then the killer has to be a woman. Or have a woman accomplice."

"Well, naturally. So obvious no careful note has been made of it. But it always did take two to dance the waltz. Maybe she's just the bait. The killing happens after."

"One thing for sure. You'll find out. They can count on that. Look at the way you cleared up the missing supplies."

"Don't be so sure on that. Carlson said there were others involved. Until I find out who they are, it can still go on."

"Nothing to it. Eli Holten will triumph in the—"

"Ssssshuh!" Eli interrupted.

"What? What is it?"

"Listen."

In the distance, cattle bawled and faint voices yipped in reply. Aching with the need of release, yet resigned to learning what he could, Eli hurriedly began to dress. Jenny did likewise.

"You wait here. I want to get a look."

Five minutes later Eli saw them. Seven men, all white, worked a mixed herd of some thirty-seven head of cattle. The cows showed rib bones and a general gauntness that indicated to Holten that they had to be Indian beef. The direction of travel was away from the agency, and the herders appeared too cautious to be anything but rustlers. Swiftly Eli returned.

"Trouble. There's some white men rustling agency cattle. I—I've got to go after them."

"What about us?" Jenny asked plaintively, every bit as in need as he.

"W-we'll have to wait, damn it. It may be too long before I get another chance like this."

"Do you have to?"

Eli considered his tender parts. "I do."

Gingerly Eli adjusted his throbbing testicles to the saddle and headed off on Sonny to stalk the herd.

Chapter 9

Late afternoon twilight filled the lodge where Crazy Horse sat with four men. *Is it wise to trust the words of this trader's son?* Crazy Horse pondered on it as he studied the flat, expressionless face of Big Bat Pourier. Would the bargain be kept? Crazy Horse doubted that very much. Still, it had become obvious that he would eventually have to give up the free life of a hostile. Every moon the *wasicun* grew more numerous, more pushy and demanding. Then there was also his wife to consider. Methodically, Crazy Horse began to pack the short pipe.

Mild bitterness touched him as he recalled the disgrace of the "Shirt Taking Away," which had compelled him to use the short pipe ever since. The demanded removal of his sign of greatness had not lessened his medicine, nor had it really deprived him of many important followers. It had been done, he suspected, as a sop to Red Cloud's feelings. Would it be an insult, he wondered, to pass the small pipe to this emissary of the Bad Faces? Probably, though it would doubtless be a worse one to offer no smoke at all to Big Bat Pourier, who also claimed to speak with the voice of Three Stars, the one called Crooked by the whites. Swiftly, Crazy Horse decided which way to do it.

Drawing deeply, Crazy Horse dedicated the pipe and passed it to He Dog. He Dog did likewise, took a deep draw, and sent it on to Little Hawk, who in turn gave it to Big Bat. Besides being in the Bad Faces' camp, Big Bat was a nephew of Red Cloud, who hated Crazy Horse more implacably now than ever before. Little Big Man received the smoke next, then returned it to Crazy Horse. All the while, Crazy Horse contemplated the alternatives.

He Dog, his *hunkaye*, his brother by choice, would have him stay out and risk the safety of the helpless ones, Crazy Horse knew. That was only because He Dog didn't have the responsibility of making the choice.

Little Hawk was another matter. That one understood the burden of a leader. In his heart, Little Hawk would want to stay out. But he would do the wisest thing when it came time.

Big Bat? Again, who knew what motivated these traders' sons? One half part of Big Bat was white. Would it be that portion which held his heart? Yet, Big Bat had openly acknowledged that there would be some glory for the man who had "talked Crazy Horse in." Lastly, he considered Little Big Man.

There was no doubting here. The fierce little warrior, even lesser in stature than Crazy Horse, would fight to the last woman and child with never once a thought to the future. Would his personal loyalty to the man he adored survive the "going in"?

Crazy Horse examined his position, weighed the limited options. Like a spectre, the image of Black Shawl, his wife, rose in his reflections.

"Wife of many winters," Crazy Horse sent his thoughts winging to her, "Crazy Horse knows you are dying of the coughing sickness."

Should he stand by his original demand for a

separate agency to hold his people? Or should Black Shawl be granted one last visit to her people, the Brules, hostages to Three Stars at the Spotted Tail agency? Tall Bear had said there would be a white medicine man for them. Would Bear Coat actually have this promised medicine man at the new agency in the north? Well, there would be one already where Red Cloud resided.

"It is always a hard thing, to know what trail is best for the people," he began by way of opening his talks with Big Bat.

"You got back sooner than I thought," Duncan McAllister greeted Walter Lehman.

"Lot of soldiers ridin' around," Lehman replied. "Damn it, I don't like it. We ought to lay low for a while."

"Oh, I quite agree. Here, spread this around among your boys and let's go in for a drink."

McAllister handed Lehman a wad of bills and gestured toward the corrals.

"They'll fatten nicely with spring coming on. Then out with the rest. Yes, I predict an extremely good year for us, partner."

Far up on a hillside, Eli Holten lay quite still as he observed the arrival of the cattle at the Box M through a brass telescope. He could not hear the words spoken, but the cordial welcome was plain enough. His stomach ached with the emptiness of a three-day ride without provisions, save for some buffalo jerky and water. He had watched the previous night, while the rustlers had built small, smokeless fires and heated running irons to convert the brands to that of the Box M. When the two men, obviously in charge, left the yard, Eli followed their

84

movements to the big front door. Then he shifted his field of vision back to the herd.

Carefully he committed to memory certain animals with outstanding markings. Even in among other cattle, the fresh scars of their altered brands stood out clearly. Next he studied the men once more, satisfying himself he could recall each of them when the time came to identify the rustlers. Finally he collapsed the brass tube and carefully disentangled his hat from the bushes, where it had served as a shade for the objective lens, and backed downhill, out of the stand of sumac.

"Easy, Sonny. That's a good boy. We've got a long way to go," Holten spoke softly to his horse at the foot of the knoll.

Casting a backward glance at the rise that screened off his view of the ranch, he swung into the saddle and touched spurs to Sonny's flanks. At a slow walk, which he stretched into a steady canter, Eli rode off to gather reinforcements.

Hein-mot Too-ya-la-kekt and Lieutenant David Perry sat together outside Joseph's lodge, laughing together. The scene, not an unusual one to either Joseph or Perry, seemed peaceful enough, albeit the lodge had been constructed hastily of brush and boughs outside the confines of Fort Lapwai. Chief Joseph and his people had stopped for a few days at the troop cantonment so that the Nez Percé leader could visit with the officers.

While they feasted each other, a report came in that he, Jospeh, and his band were at that moment harrassing the white residents of Wallowa Valley, the citizens urgently requesting that troops be sent to avert an imminent massacre. Angered by this calumny, Joseph made bitter remarks, to which Perry answered with ease and humor.

"It's a good thing you're here. I'll wire General Howard and inform him of the falsity of this report. Actually, you can't take it too hard. The farmers up there are part-time stage robbers, rustlers, and other such riffraff. As it happens they've had a fine harvest and are stuck with surplusses. Their own scheme is to get us up there in a hurry so we have to purchase their hay and grain at inflated prices."

"They are criminals, then?" Joseph inquired in his passable English.

"More or less. Many are, anyway."

"Hummm. It is a fine example of what our people can expect from our new white neighbors, eh?"

"Sorry to say, I'm afraid you're right. Unfortunately, I have no control over these people. In fact, most of the more undesirable elements have already been run out of the settlements by regulators."

"When we saw our new *homeland*," Joseph countered with a tone of bitterness, "I was astounded to find white men even there. The land is supposed to be ours. All of it. Yet there they sprawl, bodies unwashed and stinking, careless dwellings constructed in ugly clearings. Their cattle eating the graze for our horses. I do not wish this new *homeland*."

"There's little we can do about it, Chief Joseph," Perry responded. "The orders came from above."

"These criminals are on our land. Why can't you remove them?"

"I . . . I can try. I'll make a report, based on the fact you couldn't possibly have been there, and see if General Howard will authorize me to remove them."

"This would be funny, if it weren't so serious."

"We started by laughing, Joseph, don't you remember?"

"Yes. Yes, we did. I only hope that you and I will be able to continue to laugh together."

Humming softly, the magnetic coils of the telegraph machine in the office at Fort Randall indicated that a message went through the line for another station. Bell's Harmonic Telegraph worked perfectly, the operator assured Eli Holten.

"Wish he'd stuck to that, instead of pokin' around with sending the human voice by wire," the horse-faced telegrapher added.

"What's this about?"

"Alexander Graham Bell. He's succeeded in transmitting the human voice over a telegraph wire. He's callin' his contraption the telephone. What he's doin' is puttin' me out of a job. Lord, why does anyone want to talk in someone's ear from a long way away? Telegraph's good enough. You can reach anywhere you'd want with it."

"Oh? What if I had to send a message to someone far off, say in Florida?"

"Easy as anything. Hell, I could send a telegram for you all the way to London, over in England. They got a cable now, buried on the bottom of the Atlantic Ocean, carries telegraph wires to the other side."

Eli found himself blinking in surprise. That was something he definitely didn't know. Like Bell and his new invention. Too much happened too fast in parts of the world he only infrequently heard about. A doctor named Pasteur was even working on a cure for hydrophobia, he'd heard only the previous year.

"Got another one of them last night."

"How's that?" Eli asked, aware his thoughts had led him astray of the conversation.

"Another soldier killed. Like the others, stabbed in the back and throat slit. *Zziiiit!* Wuuup! That's my call."

The operator turned to his instrument and noted down the coded letters clattering out of the wooden case of the ticker. He finished in a short while, sent his confirmation, and returned to the counter, a yellow pad in his hand.

"That was your reply. Or, rather, not a reply. 'Miles is in the field, unable to authorize required force until his return.' That's what it says."

"Damn. Thank you anyway."

"Who's gonna pay for this?"

"The army."

"How nice for me," the sour telegrapher responded to Eli's departing back.

Doctor Thaddeus Molson looked up from his desk at the tall, lean man in buckskins. He blinked, removed a pince-nez and scrubbed at the lenses, then returned the device to his face. Then he worked his mustache-framed mouth into shape to form words.

"Ah, yes. Eli Holten, from Fort Rawlins. How may I help you?"

"As post surgeon, did you have an opportunity to examine the body of this last soldier killed, Doctor Molson?"

"Why, yes, I did. Terrible thing. Like all the others, a lateral incision, in the form of a puncture, of some four inches toward the midline of the left rhenal body and another deep one through the thorax and carotid artery. Died in a flash."

"Did you happen to ascertain whether or not he had engaged in intercourse shortly before or at the time of death?"

"Ummm. Interesting you should mention that. I had a directive from Colonel Miles to that effect a

88

short while ago."

"And I'm looking into these killings at the colonel's request," Eli informed him.

"Well then, I'll say this. I looked and he had. Can't tell you with whom or whether more than one time, or even, God forbid, if at the moment of death. What sort of ghoul would choose a moment like that to strike?"

"There are, as you should know, being a doctor, some strange people in the world," Eli answered.

"That I know, young man. Does that do anything toward clearing up the little mystery?"

"Only to add another to the list," Eli responded regretfully.

With nothing to do but wait for Miles to come in and send him the needed troops to close down the rustling operation, Eli considered, he might as well return to Fort Thompson and take a swing at the murder ring. It had to be squaws, he reflected regretfully.

Which made his plan all the more dangerous.

Chapter 10

A bluish haze distorted distant objects in the dishlike valley that held Fort Thompson. The result of warm spring sun and the previous night's rain, the shimmering mist concealed from Eli Holten the conical lodges of the Sioux strays who had gathered outside the confines of the military post. He rode nearly upon them before the yips of dogs and squeals of children reminded him of their presence. Their number, as usual, had increased in his absence. The Red Cloud agency was only over a few hills, yet there were always a few who preferred to huddle close-by the army. Eli entered the fort and reported in, only to discover that Miles remained in the field.

On his own, he turned Sonny in to the stable for a long and deserved rest, then sought out a friend from the previous winter's campaign. Corporal Will Tanner had proven himself a reliable man in more than one circumstance. Now Eli had a plan he felt the young noncom would be interested in. He found Tanner off duty and in the partitioned-off NCO section of the bar at the sutler's store.

"Will, I've been going over what is known about the killings," he began with scant preamble. "It's brought me to the conclusion that there is a regular murder ring. One made up of squaws. Does that make sense?"

Tanner blinked owlishly and drained his schooner of beer. "That's an interesting proposition, all right, if you can find a reason."

"I think I have that, too. The soldiers are being killed for their weapons. At least the person who set up the whole plot had that as the main purpose. What I proposed to do is get ahold of the women involved. It shouldn't take too much effort to get out of them the name of whoever got the ring going."

"Where do I fit into this, Eli?"

"You, my friend, are going to be the bait," Holten told Tanner. "We'll set it up for tomorrow night. That saloon outside the post that uses Sioux girls to, ah, 'entertain' the troops. If you get the come-on, follow through. I'll be close behind."

"I hope it's good and close, Eli. Those fellas got right proper dead, you know," Tanner observed.

"It'll all work out, Will. The worst that might happen is that you get your wick wet."

Tanner brightened. "Then I'm your man. We'll give it our best."

"In the event the girls are working with someone inside the army, we'll meet here, make a show of wanting more action, and move on to the saloon."

A frown creased Tanner's brow. "You think maybe it's one of ours?"

"We can't reject the possibility out of hand. Now, ah, enjoy your beer. I've got something else that, er, needs doing."

Holten rose and started for the door, legs somewhat wide-spread, favoring the numb ache that radiated from his loins. Each step reminded him of his interrupted love-making when he'd spotted the stolen agency cattle. The dull pain became an agonizing throb by the time he reached Jenny's small cabin. No

91

light showed this early in the day, and he found the door unlatched. With eager anticipation, he burst inside.

To find the place empty. A note lay on the table, a careless lead scrawl on the back of a shipping invoice. *Dearest Eli*, it read. *I had a short haul to the Red Cloud agency. Won't be back until after dark, day after tomorrow. Love, Jenny.*

A groan broke from Eli's lips. The message had been dated that day. Unable to endure the stones much longer, Eli headed for the saloon he'd mentioned to Tanner. Perhaps he could get a quickie in the back room, he considered. And it would help in making believable their visit the next night. At least, he reasoned it that way as he shuffled out to the eastern side of Fort Thompson.

Half a dozen civilian idlers lined the bar in a tumbledown structure of lodgepole pines and canvas. At a table, four soldiers and a nattily dressed civilian played poker. With a once-white apron spread over the expanse of a large though solid belly, a bullet-headed man with flowing walrus mustache presided over the drinks. His pudgy, beringed hand deftly drew beer from a huge keg and he dispensed shots of off-color whiskey without wasting a drop. Eli crossed to a place along the mahogany that afforded him space to each side. He laid his new .45–60 Winchester '76 on the bar and ordered a beer.

"Just get in?" the apron inquired.

"Yep. Been lookin' around down south," Eli lied smoothly.

Without artifice, the barkeep looked Eli up and down, noted the tall, lean hardness and clear, steady eyes. He extended a big hand. "Name's Justin Burdette. You lookin' for work?"

"Could be," Eli responded cautiously. "Depends on what it is."

"I could use a good man. Someone who's taken a few knocks and can handle his fists. You look to be the sort."

"Ummm. You want someone who can keep order, that it?"

"Yep. That and take charge of the till. Sort of keep my barmen honest."

"What about these?" Eli asked, nodding to a quartet of young Sioux women, dressed in calico.

"Oh, you'd get a percentage on what they make, same's me. You'd see they handed over the money after each trick was turned, that none of the sol'jer boys got too rough with them. Girl with a marked-up face don't do much business. Well, what do you say?"

"I'll have to think on it. Right now I got a powerful thirst needs wettin' down."

Burdette shrugged and walked away. The moment he left, one of the bar girls sauntered over. She smiled, a wide, toothy grimace. A pink arrowtip of tongue wet her lips.

"You buy Grass Song drink?" she managed in accented English.

"Well, aaaah . . . sure, why not?"

After the ritual purchase had been completed, Grass Song moved in closer. "I not see you before time."

"I've not been here before."

"You like Grass Song?"

"I like," Eli answered, his pressing need a roaring demand by now.

Boldly, Grass Song reached out and grasped Eli's semierect organ. "Maybe you want put this deep

93

inside Grass Song, no?"

"I, ah, well, yeah, I would. That could be nice."

She continued to knead his swelling maleness, Eli noted pleasedly, though her eyes kept darting to the shiny new Winchester. Of the remaining girls, he saw nothing. One had departed with a randy cowman and the others were nowhere near. Eli spared a moment's regret for his unfaithfulness to Jenny and then joyfully surrendered himself to the game.

"We go quick time here, one dollar. You come with me for good, long time, two dollar."

Somehow, despite his preoccupation with his sexual compulsion, Holten sensed he had a portion of the murder scheme right at hand. If a similar situation developed at the Red Cloud agency and Fort Randall, he'd be sure of it. The thing was not to tip his hand too soon. He fished in his pocket to retrieve a coin.

" 'Fraid I've only got a dollar, so it'll have to be a quickie."

Grass Song frowned in disappointment, as would any whore deprived of half her fee, Eli noted. It meant nothing really. Yet he recalled that she had at first exhibited as much interest in his rifle as in his rigid tallywhacker. Eli handed her the silver dollar and nodded to Burdette. He scooped up his Winchester and let Bird Song lead him by the other hand.

Beyond a beaded glass curtain, they entered a small, dark alcove. Only a low light, from a lamp with a blue-painted chimney, radiated from a niche in the back wall. Bird Song hitched up her skirt, to reveal a small, hairless mound, with an almost virginal cleft, and the unformed contours of a girl barely in her teens. She tucked the hem in at her waist and patted the rawhide cover of a horsehair-stuffed bench along one wall. Then she reached for his fly.

Buttons undid easily under her deft touch. An uncomfortable feeling filled Eli. He could not shake the impression that he had stumbled into the murder ring, and yet he could not visualize the killings being down here and the bodies moved later. Caution and lust warred in his powerful frame.

Lust won as Grass Song cupped his tender scrotum and squeezed gently, while her other small hand stroked his long, upcurved shaft. She bent slightly and licked the glistening tip. Eli groaned.

"You big man. Me take this way first, *ceazin*. It good. You like berry much."

Her feathery lips fluttering over his heated organ crumbled the last walls of Eli's resistance. Grass Song slurped and gulped. Pleasure radiated through Eli's rangy body. His nipples hardened and he gasped repeatedly when the young Sioux did remarkable things to his sensitive flesh. His ardor rose to an incandescent level.

"Now," he croaked harshly. "Let me take you now."

In a flash, Grass Song splayed herself on the padded bench, legs wide-spread and welcoming. Her tiny cleft opened to reveal a glistening of readying moisture that flowed over the pink petals. Eli knelt between her raised knees and then approached the tunnel of joy with his surging engine.

When it cleaved her, she cried out in terrible pain. She writhed and attempted to escape the incredible bulk that threatened to split her purse open like a ruined plum in high summer. Unable to bridle his stampeded emotions, Eli bore in, unmindful of her discomfort.

"No, no," she pleaded. "Not so much."

Pierced by her pleas, Eli slacked off. He recalled with what ease Samantha or Susanna—girls not yet of an age with Grass Song—had taken him to the hilt and wondered over it. Immediate shame at his ferocity turned the scout's face scarlet. Slowly he eased into her slippery passage. Grass Song moaned and cooed now, his warmth filling her with joy that transcended her early discomfort. Experimentally she thrust with her hips.

Eli responded with a swinging gyration that set off bells in her head. Burdette wanted these liaisons to last not more than ten minutes, but as she adjusted to the hugeness of her new customer, Grass Song wished it would go on for the rest of the day. Primed to the point of steaming from the ears, it took Eli little time to hurtle up the incline to a massive completion that had him rocking and quaking with violent shudders and left his partner a quivering, squealing mass of overstimulated nerves.

"Y-you fast," Grass Song gasped.

"Far too fast."

A shy smile lighted her dark features. "We have time. You want go again?"

Compelled by a body nowhere near repletion, Eli adjusted their position to one of greater comfort and slowly started to stroke in and out. "Sure, why not? Is it gonna cost me?"

"For you, no. You like stallion. Sooo big. Make me happy."

"I'll make you happy from now on, if you'll let me," Eli promised.

A thunderclap of noise and excitement from out in the saloon clawed at his drifting attention. "He's come in!" a voice shouted.

"Crazy Horse?" queried a soldier.

"No. But Little Hawk did. He's at the Red Cloud agency," came the reply.

An excited babble of voices broke out: bets being

made whether this meant the dread Crazy Horse would also take the way of peace, dire predictions of another uprising, with the peaceful Sioux being drawn away from the reservation, as they had been the spring of the Custer disaster, some expressing the opinion that Miles had already been massacred and that the perpetrators sought safety on the agency. Try as he might, not even Holten's prodigious carnality could be sustained in light of this.

Red-faced and confused, he wilted deep within. Grass Song tried clever tricks with the muscles that surrounded her passage, to no avail. Embarrassed, Eli withdrew his flaccid member and returned it to his trousers. He would have to look into this. He muttered some inconsequential words of apology and condolence, then departed rapidly, lest he hear raucous laughter behind him.

"Sure 'nuff," Captain Kleiner assured Eli Holten twenty minutes later. "Little Hawk and about thirty hostiles rode in yesterday. We've been over roundin' up their extra arms and ammunition, left a little for hunting. Also their war ponies. They didn't like it, but said Tall Bear—that's you isn't it?—had told them that would happen."

"I did. Glad they didn't go wild over it. I ought to get out there, talk to Little Hawk," Eli replied.

"Good idea. Way I figure it, they came in to test the waters for Crazy Horse, see if everything would be safe and peaceful."

"The very reason I want to be there to talk with Little Hawk. I'd like to draw a horse. Sonny's worn to a nubbin. I'll be back some time tomorrow."

"Go ahead. I'll send a note with you to the stable sergeant."

"Thank you, Dan."

Less than fifteen minutes later, the buildings of Fort Thompson and the surrounding villages of whites and Indians disappeared behind a gentle rise. Holten let his mount out into a smooth, ground-devouring pace and rocked comfortably in the saddle. At least his groin no longer sent off urgent distress signals. Mild ones, a promise of rapidly returning demand, yes, but not the incapacitating misery of before his encounter with Grass Song.

Eli reached the agency two hours before nightfall. He went immediately to the resident agent and learned where Little Hawk and his people had set up. A half-hour ride brought him to the sub-chief's lodge. Little Hawk greeted him warmly and ushered him inside. They worked on the pipe for a while.

"Little Hawk, it's good to see you have come in. You should send word of your treatment to our friend Crazy Horse. When you do, however, advise him that it would be better to take Bear Coat's offer than to come here."

"Why is that? We were greeted most kindly, Tall Bear."

Eli frowned as he puzzled over how to explain the problem to Little Hawk. "There is only jealousy and hatred here for Crazy Horse. Those who would never let him have safety are here and wish only to see harm come to him. Bear Coat's words are straight. A new agency for Crazy Horse is the best answer."

"We are being feasted tonight. All of the faces hold smiles for us."

Eli reached out to grasp Little Hawk by the shoulder. "Smiles can be false, my friend. You know this."

"I . . . will think on this. We're tired of running from the soldiers. Tired of seeing our children go hungrier each moon. We want peace, Tall Bear."

"And so you shall have it. Only it is best kept if you are away from the Bad Faces. I'll leave you, friend. Enjoy this feast, but keep a watchful eye on what lies behind those smiles."

Out in the small encampment, Eli noticed one of the missing girls from the saloon. She must have learned of this event ahead of the white population and come to visit relatives, he considered. Her eyes picked him out from the aimless movement of the Oglala warriors and she locked her gaze with his. A pleasant smile crinkled the corners of her mouth. Then, with a quick flick of her obsidian orbs, she took in the Winchester .45–60. Her coy welcome became radiant.

Chapter 11

Pelting the ground with small, moccasined feet, a flock of shouting young boys swirled around Eli and re-formed on the far side. A woman yelled shrilly at them that they were the offspring of the Trickster for they had surely frightened the dog she'd been about to kill for the stewing pot. Eli Holten chuckled at this peaceful Sioux domestic scene, then, on impulse, walked directly to where the young woman stood boldly staring at him.

"I see you," he said in Lakota, by way of formal greeting.

It startled her, but she managed a murmured reply. "I see you. You were at the fort called Thompson."

"Yes. In the saloon. I am a friend of Little Hawk."

Her expression indicated she didn't believe the least bit of that. She eyed the rifle again and produced a calculated smile. "Come into my lodge."

"I am Tall Bear," Holten introduced himself.

"Mahpiya-luta," she responded.

Colored Cloud. A pretty name," Eli told her as he bent to enter the lodge.

Away from the eyes of others, she relaxed some and they conversed lightly while she prepared a horn cup of herbal tea. She had been out with the hostiles for a long time. Even before the Battle on the Greasy

Grass. Her father and husband fought bravely. Her husband, she informed Eli, had been killed in the fighting with Bear Coat Miles the previous January on Hanging Woman Creek.

"Have you any children?"

"Colored Cloud's eyes lowered. "No. I had one, a small son. He died also in that sad place."

Odd, the scout thought, she seemed not to be deeply touched by the double tragedy. When the tea boiled, Colored Cloud poured it and brought a hornful to Eli. She gathered her skirts and settled gracefully beside him in a bold and provocative manner.

"I am so lonely without a man," she stated forcefully. "Is it true you are a friend to Little Hawk?"

"I am," Eli responded.

Colored Cloud placed a small, warm hand on his thigh and began to rub gently. "I should make you most welcome then. In every way," she offered brazenly.

Her hand worked upward toward Holten's suddenly revived maleness. He felt a twinge, easily dismissed in these circumstances, and decided to see where this would lead. He gave her what he hoped would be a leer of eagerness.

Swiftly Colored Cloud moved directly to her goal and began squeezing firmly on his thickening member. "I need a man to keep me happy. Do you like me?"

"You're pretty, young, make good tea, and seem to like what I like. How could I not like you?"

"You speak in riddles, Tall Bear. Come, lay back and let me ease your tensions. I can be very good to you."

"I-I'm sure you can."

Eli cooperated and brightened at the whispery

sound of her calico dress sliding over her skin. It came off, to reveal a pale bronze body, unmarked by scars, pinkly glowing with aroused passion. She bent low and rubbed her cheek against his.

"Be good to me, Tall Bear, and fill me with this mighty lance." Another persistent squeeze put Eli beyond caution.

Not too much, though, that he failed to take notice of the solid lump in the sleeping robes against which he reclined. As Colored Cloud lowered herself over him, he felt it and determined it to be a rather large, heavy butcher knife. She quickly released his rigid pole and sank upon it with hunger. Impaled through her cleft, she surged and swayed, drawing her partner deep into the silken folds of nature's divine trap. Fully aroused, Eli began to participate with his own earnest effort.

Happiness bubbled up inside Colored Cloud and she experienced a moment of regret, suddenly displaced by a tremendous climax, before she slumped forward and reached for the knife. Holten caught her by the hand and pinned it to the ground. Colored Cloud squealed and cursed him in Lakota.

"Unkce! Wasicun unkce!" she bellowed. Then she rapidly shouted out two names.

Like furies from the pit, two more young women swarmed into the tipi, knives drawn, and launched themselves at the supine scout. Eli released Colored Cloud and rolled away to safety, while a knife thudded into the robes where his chest had been. He scissored his legs and swept one lithe young Sioux off her feet. She spat profanity at him in three languages and tried to hamstring his left leg. In the whirl of the unexpected melee, Holten recognized Grass Song as his assailant.

Urgently he drew his feet back in an attempt to get

102

them under him. Colored Cloud flew at him once more. He rapped her solidly along the right side of her jaw with his left. She uttered a soft sigh and fell on her back, the butcher knife still clutched tightly in a stabbing position. The third girl, squat, round, and ugly in comparison with these beauties, hurtled past Grass Song, only to trip over her outstretched legs and fall forward.

A harsh scream issued from her hate-twisted lips and she went limp a moment after Colored Cloud's big Green River butcher knife slid deeply into her breast. Grass Song pulled a bloody hand from under the body and wailed in horror and grief. Quickly Eli regained his feet and gathered the weapons.

"Who was she?" he asked the weeping Grass Song.

"Tazuskawin," she answered simply.

"She is dead now and all for nothing," the scout told her sternly. "Why did you do this? What caused you to take the terrible risk of murdering soldiers?"

Grass Song's lips curled in disdain. "Ant Woman brought us together. We were from different bands. All three of us had lost entire families to soldier bullets. Colored Cloud and I our husbands and children, Ant Woman her mother and father, two brothers and a little sister. We wanted to hurt, to pay back. We'd found nothing left for us in the hostile bands. We came away to live at the agency. It's worse, we find, with more of the soldiers always around. We learned to drink whiskey. We'd get some if we let the soldiers use us. We talked, decided." She shrugged and again took up weeping for the ugly young woman dead at her feet.

"It was Colored Cloud who learned we'd get money for laying on our backs for their little *cepi*. A breed got us work at the whiskey place. Of the three of us, only she and I liked that. Tazuskawin had never taken real pleasure from what a man did with her. She often said she thought she was dead down there. At least so with men. Sometimes she would lay with one of us and we'd do things she instructed us in. Then she would sigh and groan and shiver all over like a woman does when her man has been good to her."

"Who did all of the killings?"

"Ant Woman did most of them. Sometimes Colored Cloud."

"And you?"

Grass Song made a face. "Never. I liked the men filling me with their warmth. The rubbing-together felt wonderful. Tazuskawin would pull them off me and cut their throats. Then she'd spit in their faces while they bled to death. I—I was always scared."

"What about the weapons you took?"

Grass Song gave him a sly look. "They are with the hostiles."

"How did you three manage that from here?"

"The 'breed was in on the scheme with Ant Woman. She took the guns to him."

"Who is this 'breed?"

"Big Foot is how the whites call him."

Eli's eyes narrowed. "I know of him. He is an evil one."

A groan came from Colored Cloud and she feebly raised upright. "There is another long gun and a short one," she corrected Grass Song in a weak voice.

"Where are they?" Eli demanded.

Unsteadily, Colored Cloud raised to her knees, took a stick from beside the fire ring, and broke it. "These are them. Hold them until I come back."

Holten accepted the symbols solemnly. When Mahpiya-luta departed, the scout continued to question Grass Song. "Would you have killed me this

104

afternoon?"

"No. Big Foot, and the man Burdette, said we were never to take the guns or kill the soldiers in that place." She paused suddenly and formed a startled expression, her left hand over her mouth.

"Burdette's mixed up in this, too?"

"I say . . . I say too much."

"No, Grass Song. If you don't tell it all to me, you and Colored Cloud are likely to be hanged by the soldier chief at Fort Thompson."

Tears streamed down Grass Song's face. "Is it not right to revenge your murdered children? To hurt those who hurt your family?"

"Not in the manner you went about it. Or at least that's the way the white man sees it."

Colored Cloud returned with a Springfield rifle and a regulation Colt .45 revolver. These she handed to Eli Holten, who returned the sticks to her. For a long while silence continued. For Eli it became a time of soul searching. A lot of what the women had told him stirred his memory of the years he spent with the Oglala. The information they imparted would enable him to round up the men responsible for this ungodly scheme. Surely Big Foot and Burdette would hang. Need the gallows claim two more victims? He stirred uncomfortably and peered into the dim coals.

"For every wrong a debt must be paid. It is the way of the Oglala. You were wronged. You took the lives of soldiers. But that, too, was a wrong in the eyes of the whites. Where, then, would it ever stop? I am sent by Bear Coat to find out about the killings. I now know. One of you is dead. The men who profited by your doings will assuredly be hanged. It's my word as Tall Bear of the Oglala that you have paid enough with this death of Ant Woman and the information you've given me. Bear Coat shall not hear of you. But from now on you must both abide by the treaties. You must not kill more of the soldiers."

"*Waugh!*" Colored Cloud burst out. "Abide by the treaties? In the way the white man does? Our people died on land the Red Cloud Treaty says was ours until the end of time."

"No," Eli told her simply. "Keep your side as the Oglala do."

Chapter 12

Thunder rumbled off to the south and the sky had a greenish-black tinge. Eli Holten figured Fort Randall would be catching hell about then. Judging from the towering height of some of the anvil-topped clouds, there would be hail aplenty. And high winds. He paused a moment on the narrow porch outside headquarters at the Red Cloud agency and reflected on the events that had brought him here.

". . . and so the ringleader tripped and fell on a knife," Eli concluded his tale to Colonel Clark, whom the Sioux called White Hat.

Clark, in command of the detachment policing the reservation, looked at the rifle and revolver and glanced back to the scout. "Arrangements will be made to round up Big Foot and Burdette at Fort Thompson. You've done the Army a great service in breaking this ring, Mr. Holten. Too bad there's not a proper way to reward you."

"I appreciate that, sir. There's one more thing. I've a good line on the men responsible for stealing cattle from here and the Spotted Tail agency."

"Oh? I'd assumed that when the hostiles came in that would stop."

"There's a rancher down on the Niobrara who receives the beef, fattens them some, and runs them in with his own. I don't have a name as yet, but his brand is the Box M. The rustlers had changed the road brand from the Roman Four, an I and V, to the Box M a day's drive away from the agency. So there's no doubt as to who is behind it. Also, as you know, the Sioux ear-notch their cattle according to clan ownership. Those marks will be easy to identify among this feller's cattle. I need a small detachment to lead down there and arrest the men involved. When the stock stops disappearing, the Sioux'll be a lot happier. Which should make your job a bit easier, I'd judge."

"Yes, it would," Clark responded in a sad tone. "Unfortunately I'm in no position to let you have any regulars. All I can spare is an interpreter-scout named Broughier and a party of Indian police, under Woman's Dress."

"But, sir . . ."

"Johnny Broughier is a good man, Holten. The Indian police, I'm proud to say, are far above average. I trained them myself."

"It may come to a killing situation, Colonel. You know what an uproar it would create if a Sioux killed a white man."

"Just so. And I'd do it another way if I could. As it stands, you'll have to take what is offered or nothing. Crazy Horse is coming in and I need every trooper here to insure he stays."

"Crazy Horse coming here? What about the separate agency Miles promised him."

"What's a promise to an Indian?" Clark dismissed. "Even if Miles gets approval from Washington, it'll be months before the new agency can be set up. Meanwhile, Crazy Horse wants to come in, so we'll be happy to accommodate him. That's all, Mr. Holten."

"I think, Colonel, that you're making a terrible mistake. There'll be trouble. Count on it."

Another day of sunshine, that's a good thing. So ran the thoughts of Chief Hein-mot Too-ya-la-kekt as he looked out over the folded and forrested hills of the Wallowa Valley. Near each family tipi, drying racks had been erected. For a week, ending yesterday, after the storms had moved eastward, the men of his tribe had slaughtered cattle. With quick, sure strokes of their sharp knives, the women cut long, thin slices of rich, dark beef and hung them on the ladder-like frameworks to cure in the sun. More would be added today.

When the jerky reached the right stage, in another day or so, it would be dipped in a thin pulp of berries, camas bulbs, wild onions, and pepper pods, then returned to the racks to be completed with their coating. But before that, the tribe would move to the camas digging grounds and unearth those delicious knobs the gods had provided. Soon it would be the Moon of Salmon Spawning. Drying and smoking salmon would come next. Yes, if the white men left them alone, it could be a good life in the Wallowa.

"We'll kill one more cow," Joseph informed his wife, who stood beside him. "The fresh meat will be good and you need it for strength."

Smiling shyly, his woman patted her swollen belly. "It will soon be time. I'm sure it will be a son for you, my husband."

"Let's hope so . . . for your sake. It's you who's counting on it," he ended with a chuckle. "We'll feast tonight. Tomorrow the meat must be packed in bundles and taken to the camas grounds. There it can finish while the bulbs are gathered." He sighed heavily. "We won't be back here for a while, I'm certain."

"How easily you make any part of our land your home, husband."

"Do I? Yes, I suppose I can be comfortable anywhere."

"Except among the whites," came a quiet reply.

Joseph frowned. "That's true. They make our lives . . . something less than what we want them to be."

"Doctor Carver, at the mission school, would say that they 'diminish' us."

"Odd how some white words don't fit our tongues at all. Others not only fit, but fit the whites and their deeds as well. *Diminish.* Yes, I like that word."

By midday following the feast of roasted beef, the Nez Percé had prepared the bundles of meat, rounded up any loose horses not used in transportation, and started out on the trek to the camas digging grounds at Tepahlewam, where the remainder of Joseph's people already waited. Progress went smoothly through the warm, hazy late May afternoon. Joseph found his spirits rising and his outlook for their future greatly improved. Therefore he greeted a hurried messenger with a lighthearted yip of welcome when the brave rode his lathered mount to a stop beside the chief.

"War clouds are gathering, Hein-mot Too-ya-la-kekt," the rider said by way of greeting.

Joseph's good mood dissolved. "What is this? Have the whites stolen horses and cattle again?"

"No. It's worse, I'm afraid. Wallitits, one of White Bird's men, has begun his own war on the whites. Wallitits is the son of Tipiala-natzikan, who was murdered by white men. He's a very angry young man."

Frowning, his expression closed and heavy, Joseph instructed the messenger, "Tell me."

"First he killed a whiskey trader, which in itself isn't such a bad thing." At Joseph's hot flash of eye and scowl, the bringer of bad news ducked his head and refrained from editorial comment. "Then Wallitits brought his friends to see what he did. They drank up all the whiskey, then went out and killed some more whites. More warriors have joined them."

From her place beside her husband, where she overheard the grim news, Hein-mot's wife screamed in mortal anguish and began the keening song for the dead. Taken as though in a swoon, she slumped and slid from her glossy Palouse horse. Joseph leaped down beside her and examined her bulging body. Then he turned a tortured face upward to those around them.

"Sh-she's begun to deliver. Bring the women at once."

Tall grass now covered the wide, rolling, unfenced pastures of the Box M. On horseback, Duncan McAllister and Walt Lehman rode side by side through the whispering green sea of gama and buffalo grass. McAllister reined in and slapped one thigh with a large, heavy hand.

"So Crazy Horse is actually coming in. Good. We've four thousand head of cattle here. Once that bloodthirsty savage is corralled and the other reservations calm down some, we can start working to make that eight thousand."

"Duncan, I'm still antsy about the Spotted Tail agency. I'll swear that it was some Brules we saw over on the north section three days ago."

"They've waited this long," McAllister responded. "Nothing says they should be poking around now. Forget it, Walt."

"You forget, *I'm* the one who has to stick my neck out. Imagine what would happen if we got jumped by a war party."

McAllister stared bleakly over the brown backs of grazing cattle until the silence became uncomfortable. "You're right, Walt. I hadn't considered that. We could bring a regular Indian war down on us. Or get the army mixed in. So we'll lay off the agency cattle for at least six months. It means we'll grow slower, but it'll be a lot safer."

"I'll tell the boys. They'll appreciate it, I'm sure. Say! An idea just struck me. What if we land a contract with the government to supply meat to the Indians? Do we sell back their own cattle to 'em?"

Harsh and jerky, laughter rose from McAllister's chest. "That's a good one. I'm tempted, but we have to be careful about those ear notches. Better to cull out those animals at roundup and see they're shipped south to the Omaha market."

"There's more than chess that's a devious game, eh, Duncan?"

"Exactly. Now, let's ride."

Jenny Blanchard lay comfortably in the crook of Eli Holten's arm. Sated by long hours of lovemaking, the contact between their skins no longer stimulated her wildly. It only made her mildly interested in exploring some new and exciting means of arousing his passion. For a moment her thoughts touched guiltily upon Marty, exiled to the small, slant-roofed room addition Eli had attached to her cabin on the opposite side of the main room.

Poor child, he must feel rejected and unwanted, she envisioned. She had followed Eli's advice and shown him more, and more open, affection, with hugs and pats and kisses on the cheek. He literally glowed. At least he did so until those times when they stopped at Fort Thompson and Eli Holten could visit. Then Marty took on a slight hint of the sulks. Not that he rebelled or showed open hostility. Martin Richter was always impeccably polite.

That, too, bothered Jenny. What did his perfect manners mask? Did he indeed secretly lust for her body? Did he lay abed at night and play with himself and, in his daydreams, imagine that he and she were together in romantic embrace? Oooh, she'd have to stop that. It was getting her terribly warmed up. Secret, forbidden desires. Everyone had them. Eli had helped her understand that. She owed him so much. Which reminded her.

"Hey, you," she whispered in his ear. "Wake up. I want to smother you with love."

"Again?" Eli rose on one elbow and looked at the big Ingersol alarm. "It's nearly two-thirty. I have to leave in the morning bright and early."

Jenny smiled enigmatically and arranged herself in an inviting display of her charms. The effect didn't go unnoticed by Eli. A devilish grin began to spread on his lips and he bent low to cover her with kisses. He started at her toes and worked upward on one creamy, well-turned leg until he reached a spot a short distance from the juncture. Then he began again on the other. Dreamily, Jenny speculated on how nice it would be to have someone else taking one side, while Eli concentrated on the other. It would double the terribly sensual sensations that washed through her.

She squeaked in sudden delight when Eli switched to her belly, adding the tip of his tongue to the arduous efforts of his burning lips as he circled her navel, spiraling inward. A quick peek along his hard,

113

scarred body revealed the long, thick mass of his phallus standing rigidly upward from a thatch of curly blond hair. It swayed tantalizingly before her and her heart began to pound, urged on by the wonderful things he did to her. Slowly Eli covered her, his tongue slathering over her pert breasts now, the pink nipples swelling to erect readiness.

Shivers spider-legged across her skin as he closed his mouth over one nipple and began to gnaw it gently. She reached out to him and tried again the impossible task of spanning his waist with both hands. Jenny lowered one leg and he moved deftly in between. His mouth nuzzled her throat. Hungrily she reached out and wrapped trembling fingers around the mighty girth of his engorged member.

How silky! How warm and real and alive. She let her fingers caterpillar-walk up to the broad, deep red tip. Rapidly she tapped on it, like using the keys of one of those new typing machines. Eli flinched away, not in pain but in intense pleasure. Slowly Jenny guided his organ toward the moistly flowing passage at the juncture of her thighs.

Her fingers parted wisps of hair and she teased her magnificent lover for long, excruciatingly lovely moments by sliding the slightest bit of the tip up and down her cleft. Bit by bit she allowed more to penetrate beyond the outer fringes of pink. Eli moaned, and thrust powerfully with his hips.

Cunningly Jenny avoided impalement and continued her amorous torment. Eli's neck corded in the strain of holding off his completion, driven to a frenzy by the magnitude of the pleasure they shared. There! Triumph burned within him as he felt the first couple of inches delve within the firm, warm channel. Maybe, maybe now she would . . .

Jenny giggled and tightened up at the first hint of

another powerful jab. Then, of a sudden, her eyes glazed slightly, her jaw sagged, and she moaned mightily as she drove upward with her hips and hilted his burning member within her fevered purse. Time became eternity and the creaky cast-iron bedframe turned into a new universe. Blissfully the lovers rocked in the rhythm of the most ancient comfort known to man.

Chapter 13

Sunlight sparkled off the placid surface of the Niobrara River. A narrow stream of a milky brown color, like coffee with a dollop of spoon cream, it had been swollen and silted by the spring rains. The inventive, pleasant comforts of Jenny Blanchard lay a week behind at Fort Thompson. Eli Holten rode with his surly command from the Red Cloud agency. His appeal to the army at Thompson had been to no avail. Miles remained in the field. Johnny Broughier set the mood for the Indian Police.

"I ain't no gunfighter, Mr. Holten," the interpreter had told him at the outset. "I've no desire to back you in a confrontation. If they don't give up peaceable, I don't know what I'll do."

"You'll do what the army pays you to do," Holten had told him coldly. "And that includes backing me in whatever goes on at the Box M."

All the same, Eli didn't trust the half Sioux, half French-Canadian scout. Such an open admission of cowardice left little doubt. For their part, the Sioux would not aid him either. He was Tall Bear, an Oglala, and thus a member of Crazy Horse's faction. Holten pleaded with them, only to learn that Johnny had told them that the army would probably not back them up if they harmed a white man. It gave the scout pause to consider the possibility that Broughier might be connected with the rustlers. Now, already on Box M land, they were deeply committed and Eli still didn't know what his detail might do.

"There's cows over there," Eli informed the Indian policemen. "You three go over and head them our way."

"What are we looking for?" Johnny asked with ill grace.

"Sioux ear notches. Also fresh brand scars."

"There you are. That'll be proof enough."

"That's true, Johnny. Then we have to go in and arrest the men doing it."

"Why not wait for the army to do that?" Johnny inquired in a peevish voice.

"While more cattle get stolen and people go hungry?"

Johnny cast an uneasy glance at the Sioux warriors with them. "All right, all right."

Woman's Dress and his Sioux policemen worked the cattle over by the trail. Eli Holten rode along the small gather until he located three animals who did not have hair regrown over the brand mark and who also bore the ear notches. He pointed to one.

"Whose mark is that?" he asked Woman's Dress in Lakota.

Dark features flushed with angry blood. "Bad Faces," Woman's Dress rumbled.

"And that one?"

"Long Heels of the Brule," Woman's Dress answered the scout.

"Now, Johnny? Now do you believe me?" Eli demanded.

"Oh, I believe you, all right. I don't want to get myself or these men in trouble is all."

Holten's determination took a new angle. "We'll do

it your way, then, Johnny. Let's present the rancher with the evidence we have and ask him to surrender himself without a fight." With that, Eli took out his Winchester and shot the brown and white cow of the Brules. "Skin that animal and take the hide along. The backside will show the altered brand."

Twenty minutes later they came within sight of the ranch house. Careful observation indicated few people up and around the place. At Holten's direction, they rode on in. Before they passed through an open, arched-over gate, a blacksmith came from his small shed, and two figures appeared on the porch of the main house.

Duncan McAllister didn't like the looks of the approaching group. Indians for the most part, wearing blue shell jackets without insignia. Reservation police most likely. He recognized the quarter-breed Broughier, knew he scouted for Colonel Clark at the Red Cloud agency. The tall blond man at the lead was a stranger. Him Duncan liked the least. Those cold, gray eyes could bore holes through a man. He decided to reveal as little of himself as he could as he took a step forward and raised a hand in greeting.

"Something I can do for you fellers?" Duncan McAllister inquired, assuming a folksy manner of speech uncommon to him.

"Yes, sir," Eli answered levelly. "M'name's Eli Holten. I'm on loan from Fort Rawlins to Colonel Miles's command."

"Well, then, how does that involve the Box M? I'm Duncan McAllister, by the way. I own this place."

In particular I'm looking into the theft of agency beef from the Sioux, Mr. McAllister. That's what's brought us to the Box M. We've located a number of head of cattle in your herd that bear the earnotches of Brule, Hunkpapa, and Oglala Sioux clans. Their brands are fresh. Your brand, Mr. McAllister."

McAllister flushed a deep scarlet. "You have no right searching my property," he thundered.

"Wrong, Mr. McAllister. So long as there are any large hostile bands out, martial law prevails on the frontier. That means the army can go wherever it wants. I understand the Constitution as well as you, and know about warrants, and searches and seizures. It's not to my liking that the army has this power, but in this case it's served its purpose."

"What are you doing here with these savages? Get off my land or I'll set my ranch hands on you."

"Bluster isn't going to get it, Mr. McAllister," Eli responded, keeping his tone calm and yet commanding. "See this hide? We took it from a cow belonging to the Brule. My guess is there's two, maybe three hundred head of Indian cattle on your spread. That could get sticky for you and everyone concerned. Now, I'll grant you that a number of strays could have found their way clear down here from the Spotted Tail agency. Or you might have innocently purchased a few head from rustlers without realizing it.

"But not three hundred. Besides, I trailed thirty-some head here, led by that man standing behind you, not three weeks ago. Now, we can make our report, and the army will eventually come down here and arrest you all. Or . . ."

"Eh? What are you getting at?" McAllister's eyes narrowed. He tried not to reflect on his face the knowledge that some half a dozen of his hands had now formed a loose half-circle behind the intruders. Quick-minded, he worked a note of shrewdness into his voice.

"You want a piece of the action? Is that it?"

Eli turned partway in the saddle and spoke in

119

Lakota. "He thinks I'm looking for a bribe." Laughter answered him from the ranks of Indian police. Then to McAllister, he said, "No. Just a little gentlemen's agreement. What I want, Mr. McAllister, is for you to stop stealing the Indians' food supply for all time in the future. Also to round up those cattle you have on your ranch and return them. In exchange for that, we'll forget all about the legal troubles that could come out of this."

"You expect me to believe that?"

"My word on it."

"What about these others?" McAllister demanded.

Right then, Johnny Broughier raised both hands and spoke in a wheedling voice. "Me and these Indian po-lice are not part of any agreement you make with Holten, Mr. McAllister. We're not backin' his play at all." He, too, had noted the gathering of armed men.

Shit! There goes the whole game, Eli thought disgustedly. He watched a broad smile spread on McAllister's face. Sickened, Eli realized the precarious position he now held.

"That leaves you sort of alone, Holten. I could shoot you down and these fellers would swear it never happened. Take a look around. I've enough men covering you now that none of you would get out of here alive. However," he went on, assuming his usual manner of speaking, "I respect your position, Mr. Broughier. Your word is good to me. I would suggest that you have a meaningful discussion with Holten and persuade him to see the light. *I don't like threats.* What I do is no business of the army, and none at all of a two-bit civilian scout. Convince him of that, Mr. Broughier."

Outflanked and outgunned, Eli tasted the bitter bile of defeat. He slowly backed Sonny into the group of Sioux, then turned and gave the signal. Together they galloped out of the ranch yard before McAllister could decide to turn his men loose on them.

Dressed in the last of his fading finery, wrapped in an agency blanket of bright red and yellow, with blue diamond pattern, Chief Red Cloud went out from the reservation to greet the arrival of Crazy Horse. An old man now, he was far from the firebrand who had engineered the Wagon Box and Fetterman fights and won for his people the best, and longest kept, treaty from the whites. With the years his glory had faded, like his once-bright war bonnet and ceremonial trappings. New stars had risen among the people. One of them, Red Cloud thought with loathing, was Crazy Horse. Along with Red Cloud came the agency loafers and idle warriors.

This cavalcade met the approaching hostiles outside Fort Robinson. Many laughed and cheered and waved branches of sage as the stern-faced Oglala trotted wordlessly between a double file of them. General Crook and his staff sat their mounts to one side, and the demonstration prompted him to remark:

"My God, this is no surrender, it's a triumphant march."

"We'll see how long that lasts," his executive officer replied confidently.

It had been decided that Fort Robinson would be the ideal location for Crazy Horse's induction into agency life. At sharp commands from the soldiers, the Oglala dismounted. Under the hard eyes and ready guns of the army, they marched forward to a hastily erected pavilion, where Crook, Colonel

121

Clark, and the civilian agent Arthur Howard sat on camp chairs. There the final ritual of surrender was enacted.

One by one the followers of Crazy Horse relinquished their firearms and precious ponies. The former lay in a growing pile to the left of the observers, the latter had the reins handed over to soldiers, who led them a short distance to a rope corral. At the end of the procession came Crazy Horse. He had no sooner laid down his arms and made a sign of acknowledgment to power than Howard rose, smiling, and spoke to Red Cloud's faction in Lakota.

"Come forward, my friends, and help yourselves."

Laughing and shouting again, though now with a smirking quality, the ne'er-do-wells of the agency surged up and loaded down with the possessions of the newly subjugated Oglala. Anger burst in Crazy Horse's breast when he realized why so many of his former enemies had been so anxious to witness his capitulation, and saw the betrayal by the whites. He took a threatening step forward.

"No! This is not as stated by Bear Coat Miles," he exclaimed hotly.

"Take your place, Crazy Horse," Colonel Clark barked. "Miles isn't here, as you can see. Henceforth you are subject to our wishes, not his."

Sadly, Crazy Horse turned to face his people. He raised his arms and cried out with the lament of so many who went before him. "There is no honor here. The *wasicunpi* lied to us. I have led you astray. If it were in our power, I would say for us to go home."

"That's enough of that," Howard snarled. "Get him out of here."

White Hat Clark looked up and his eyes locked with those of Little Big Man. They each made a curt nod that seemed to imply agreement with the words Colonel Clark spoke to General Crook.

"There's going to be trouble. I can taste it."

Big Foot drove a huge fist into a small cask, shattering it. Burdette's place had been closed, the man arrested by soldiers, and they looked now for him. How could it have happened? At once he left the small storage shed behind the saloon outside Fort Thompson and kicked the ribs of his pony until the animal reached a full gallop. He headed directly for the agency. Sintiega-leska, Spotted Tail, would know what had happened. If not, the women could be found and made to talk.

He arrived amid the flurry of excitement over the coming-in of Crazy Horse. Feasts were being prepared for friends and relatives among the former hostiles. Big Foot went unnoticed by the vigilant soldiers. He received less than a cordial greeting from Spotted Tail and no information at all. He set out to find Colored Cloud or one of the others.

Poor Colored Cloud grew immobile with fright when she saw Big Foot stalking in her direction. Her lips trembled and she whimpered when he grabbed her roughly by the upper arm and frog-marched her off to the privacy of a clump of birch.

"What happened?" he demanded roughly.

"We were caught," she said simply.

"You're not telling me everything, Colored Cloud."

"It's like I said. A man came from the army, he suspected something, and caught us. Ant Woman is dead. Grass Song has gone back to her people."

Big Foot struck her a backhand blow across the face. "How much do they know?"

"Only . . . only that we were the ones," Colored

Cloud replied evasively.

"Burdette is arrested. They know more than that."

Big Foot hit her again and Colored Cloud went to her knees. He struck her over and over with his fists, then kicked her in the stomach. Spewing bile from her burning throat, the battered woman lay on her side, choking on sobs. Still Big Foot did not relent.

"Tell me everything," he demanded.

Slowly, with more punches between answers, Colored Cloud revealed the extent of what Eli Holten had been told. Big Foot asked each question several times. When she finished he struck her once more. A small bone in her neck broke with an audible snap.

Colored Cloud made a liquid rattle and quivered for a few moments, then went slack as her eyes began to glaze in death. Grunting indifferently, Big Foot wiped his hands and walked away without a glance at his victim.

Chapter 14

Sunlight dappled the leaves of cottonwood and blackjack. Birds made midday joyous with song. Dust rose in thick billows from the parade ground at Fort Thompson, where three companies of infantry labored at dismounted drill. From a distance, the absence of swarms of men indicated that Miles, with half of the infantry and the Seventh Cavalry, remained in the field. Still disgusted with his failure and the performance of the Indian police, Eli Holten arrived well ahead of his party. At headquarters he was ushered in to see Colonel Clark, who had himself just returned from the Red Cloud agency.

"I had them cold," the scout angrily told the colonel. "A fresh hide, brand altered. I'd learned from you and Major Twiss that the last consignment of cattle had used the Roman Four as a road brand. There it was, relatively fresh, with the Box M done over it with a running iron."

"You actually confronted this, ah, Duncan McAllister?"

"Right. And that's when Johnny Broughier turned tail. McAllister had half a dozen men on hand, all armed, and we weren't ready for anything. Worse, the Indian police were afraid of what might happen if they harmed a white."

"We have his name now, and a location. The matter can be dealt with when Miles returns. Speaking of which, I've had orders for you from Nelson for the last three days. Here they are."

"Thank you." Eli took the sheet of paper and opened it, slitting the wax seal with a thumbnail.

Past the usual salutation, Miles got directly to the meat. *Subject scout, Eli Holten, is ordered hereby to immediately join the command. We have made a brushing contact with Gall and are in pursuit. You are to lead the contingent of Crow scouts at Fort Thompson to a rendezvous on the Milk River, at a point within two miles of the mouth of the river.*

Not one to waste words, the scout considered. "I'll leave the rustlers to you, then, Colonel. Miles is in hot pursuit of Gall and his band, and wants me to take the Crow scouts and join him on the Milk."

"Damn. We need those troops here to insure Crazy Horse and his wild men are pacified. Oh, well, Gall and Sitting Bull have the last two bands out. If Miles gets them we have 'em all. Be sure you take ample provisions. I've a strong feeling Miles will have little to spare. Remember what happened to our esteemed General Crook in '76?"

Eli allowed himself a small smile. Clark could be human after all. He made his next stop at Jenny's cabin.

"She iss not here," Martin Richter informed him, his small boy lips forming a pout.

"When will she be back?" Eli asked politely.

"Neffer for you," Martin nearly shouted. "Not if I haff my vay."

His last conversation with Jenny recalled itself. Here, clearly, was a case of both jealousy and childlike resentment of someone who claimed the affection of a parent. Eli placed an arm on the boy's

126

shoulder and the boy stiffened. Ignoring it, the scout pushed his way inside. He led Martin to a chair and took one for himself.

"Marty, Marty, there's something you have to understand."

"I under-ah-stand vell enough."

"That's just the point. You don't. You're starting to see Jenny as a second mother, right?"

"*Ja,*" the lad answered cautiously.

"That's good. She loves you and would probably try to adopt you if she thought she had a chance. Her occupation and way of life aren't exactly what the do-gooders and bleeding-hearts see as desirable in an adoptive parent. All the same, she looks on you as a son. That doesn't mean she doesn't have, and shouldn't have, another sort of love for someone else. You had a family, didn't you?"

"*Ja.* Of course. Vat has dat to do mit it?"

"Your mother loved you, didn't she? And your father?"

"*Ja.*"

"Yet they also had another sort of love between each other, I'm sure you knew that."

Martin's eyes gleamed. A shy smile formed. "*Ja.* Dot's how babies are made."

"Well, I wasn't exactly ready to get into it that far as yet," the scout dissembled. "You're right, though. Jenny loves you, but she also loves me. But *not in the same way.*"

Now Martin nodded vigorously, as though in confirmation of some unspoken statement. His big eyes looked quizzically at Eli. Suddenly at a loss for words, the scout made useless, fumbling gestures with his big hands. Impulsively he reached out. Martin hesitated, his eyes filled, and he sprang forward to be embraced by Eli.

127

"If there's room in her heart for both of us, couldn't there be room in yours for her and me? Because she loves me, doesn't mean you *have* to hate me."

Wet salt tears soaked into the scout's whipcord jacket. "I don't! I don't hate you. I—I . . . I don't know how I should feel about you a-a-an' I'm sorry."

Deeply moved by this gush of emotion and uncertain how to deal with it, Eli could only pat the small boy's fine, black hair and murmur soothing, meaningless sounds. Martin held on tightly until his sobs subsided. Then he looked up, his chin quivering. Shyly, his long lashes lowered, Martin raised up on tiptoe and gave Eli a light, fleeting kiss on the cheek.

"Dat's how Jenny kisses me. Only . . . only longer and, er, *warmer*." His embarrassment sent Martin into giggles.

The three of them had dinner together. Then Martin went happily off to his room with a new book Jenny had brought him from a publisher's drummer on the steamboat. Eli and Jenny sipped whiskey-laced coffee and made small talk for about an hour. Then, with looks of mutual longing, they headed for the bed.

Naked and snuggled beneath the covers, Eli eased himself into Jenny's welcoming passage. With a languidness that bordered on no motion at all, he stroked into her, creating a new sort of excitement. How nice it would be, he speculated, if the rest of his life could be like this. Deep-seated fires caught at last and the ease turned to energetic eagerness. After the final, ecstatic explosion, they lay back, assured in each other's happiness, and talked quietly.

"Martin seemed somehow different. He didn't make any fuss at all when we sent him off for the night," Jenny observed.

"A new book's a fascination to a boy with an eager mind," Eli answered lightly. "Besides, we had a long talk this afternoon."

"Oh? About what?"

"You," Eli said with a kiss on her nose.

"What did you tell him?"

"I told him that if he didn't straighten out, I'd scalp him alive and then feed his pecker to Miz Halloran's goose."

"Eli!"

Laughing, Eli hugged her to him. "Only kidding, love. I think," he went on, seriously, "I think he sees things in a better light. We talked, he did a little crying, and then we did a little hugging. After that he declared me to be his best pal."

"You'll never stop amazing me, Eli. You're wise in so many ways."

"I love being admired for my brain."

"Rat! I'll show you what you're admired for," she challenged with a quick grab to his fully erect organ.

"Oh-ho, just an old stud horse, eh?"

"We-l-l . . . not so *old*, thank God."

"Shall we?"

"When have I ever said no?"

Fourteen Crow scouts sat their mounts in the darkness. They waited for Eli Holten on the far side of the parade ground, near the symbolic stone columns that represented the main gate. They didn't talk among themselves, or smoke, as would white troops, yet they wore the blue jackets and broad-brimmed campaign hats of cavalry, several with corporal's chevrons and one the point-down rockers of a staff sergeant. The remainder of their clothing consisted of leggings, breechcloths, and moccasins. Each had a large bag of provisions for man and horse tied on behind his saddle. A train of six heavy-laden pack animals stood hip-shot nearby.

"The Oglala, Tall Bear," the sergeant announced at Eli's approach, his tone one of near disgust. The Crow and Sioux did not get along.

"He is also white and a fierce fighter," a member of the ranks reminded their leader.

"To me, he's an Oglala," the sergeant snapped, then spat on the ground.

"Good morning," Eli greeted softly in the Absaroka tongue.

Mutters of surprise came from his small, temporary command. "Sergeant Tim Black-Belly," the noncom reported, with a slow, insolent salute.

"Sergeant," Eli returned dryly. "You needn't salute me. I'm a civilian. First off, you men know the country between here and the mouth of the Milk better than I. I'm going to rely on your judgment to get us there the swiftest, easiest way you can."

Tim Black-Belly raised his eyebrows. Perhaps this Oglala wouldn't be so bad after all. "We are going after Gall?"

"Yes. That's what Bear Coat is up to right now. We're to join him."

A wide, white smile spread on Tim's face. "Now that I like."

"So do I," Eli responded. "Get 'em on the road, Sergeant. We'll stop to have breakfast after it's light and no one can spot our fire."

Thirteen pairs of eyes watched the small contingent ride out of Fort Thompson and head northwest. They belonged to Big Foot and the rabble he had gathered around him. In addition to the ring of

130

murderous squaws, Big Foot employed a network of thugs, cutpurses, rollers, and road agents. These twelve constituted the most efficient of the crop. Three were black, former slaves who had drifted West and ended up in a life of crime. *Tablokala*, buffalo boys, the others—who all had some degree of Indian blood—called them. Short of temper, dull of wit, and totally devoid of moral principles, only the brute size and ferocity of Big Foot kept them in line. They looked on with eyes that gleamed with blood-lust as Big Foot pointed out Eli Holten.

"That one. We are going to follow along and, when the time is right, we kill him."

Chapter 15

An almost palpable miasma, like the mist around a waterfall, hung over the village. To the east, stars were beginning to wink out, though there was as yet no perceptible lightning of the nighttime sky. Liquor-sodden warriors lay sprawled in unexpected places. Few had managed to reach their sleeping robes. Heartsick, Chief Joseph wandered through the camp in an attempt to arouse the men. Senses reeling from one emotional shock after another, not from the white man's poison, he stumbled and moved aimlessly.

"Up, Camas Heart," he shouted to a supine warrior. "Get moving, Bringer of Thunder," he urged another bleary-eyed reveler. "Hurry, hurry, all of you."

For many days, since Wallitits and Too-hool-hool-zote had taken their war to the whites, nothing had been done directly against Joseph and his people. The camas bulbs were gathered, processed, and stored away. The main camp returned to the river-bank and made ready for the salmon. Still the white soldiers and General Howard remained out of the Wallowa Valley. For the past two days he and his brother, Ollokot, had kept camp in this place. Many of the young men who had raided with Wallitits had gathered here. They brought with them the whiskey. The result had been disaster.

"Splash them with water," Ollokot suggested gaily, his usual smile undimmed by drink.

"I'll roll them in the river." Joseph's mood changed. "We are agreed then, today as over the past two?"

"Of course, Brother. We have fasted and purified ourselves and spoken with the Spirits. We're agreed. There's only one possible conclusion. We will work for peace with all our hearts." Ollokot's eyes glowed with renewed zeal as he spoke the rest of their decision. "Or fall in battle, at one with our people."

"So we shall, Brother, so we shall," Joseph agreed with far less enthusiasm. "Help me, now, Ollokot, for our scouts have reported in. Howard's not waiting any longer. Soldiers are coming into the valley, led by my friend Lieutenant Perry. We've little time to revive these sluggards and make preparations."

Within an hour and a half, the badly hungover Nez Percé warriors revived enough to take a light breakfast. During that time, scouts came and went with news. Contrary to earlier reports, there was a stranger in command of the soldiers who numbered two full companies with their own pack train. Perry was there all right, but in command of the second half of the column. Joseph sighed with the sad knowledge he was outnumbered more than four to one.

The soldiers advanced at a steady pace. Nothing, it would seem, could discourage them. At last Joseph left off haranguing his suffering men, and walked purposefully to where six mounted headmen waited. This was his peace delegation. One of them bore a large white banner he'd prepared the previous evening after he and Ollokot had delivered their decision.

They would ride out and seek Perry. Assure him of their peaceful intent. No matter that a few individuals violated the treaty oath. The tribe wanted peace. Perry would understand, and through him, Howard. Now, with the soldiers already on their ground, they of need would go to them here.

After all, Howard would surely understand.

Lieutenant David Perry had an uneasy feeling about this foray into the Wallowa Valley. He trusted Joseph and he knew Joseph trusted him. The young officer's discomfort came from the presence of a dozen civilians with the military column. Led by Ad Chapman, they represented the white faction that so coveted the valley for their own.

Chapman was a firebrand. Perry knew he was one of those who had "manufactured" evidence of Nez Percé raids early in the spring in order to unload surplusses of hay on the army. In light of this, his presence could hardly be auspicious. Yet, Headquarters had authorized Chapman's presence, along with the others, as local guides. This, though, was not the sum total of Perry's worries.

Overall command of the expedition had been given to an officer totally unfamiliar both with the terrain and with the disposition of Chief Joseph and his band of Nez Percé. Captain William H. Boyle, formerly an aide to General Howard and just prior to that a member of the inspector general's department at Headquarters, was a stranger to the entire situation.

Boyle had recently been promoted and replaced Captain Henry M. Smith, who had died of heart ailment, as commanding officer of G Company, 21st Infantry. In this situation, command in the field of G

Company settled on Lieutenant Edward Theller, who had volunteered for the assignment. Through most of the journey, Theller had ridden with Ad Chapman's complement of "guides." Now, inside the valley, Captain Boyle accompanied the civilians, and Ed Theller had taken command of G Company.

This situation didn't sit well with Perry. When a Nez Percé woman and child had been discovered at the side of the trail, in a narrow place where it entered the valley proper, Perry had had to all but physically restrain the civilians from killing them both. Boyle, he had noted, did not interfere.

All this would soon prove academic, David Perry thought, as he glanced forward through the hazy light of early morning and saw a delegation of *Nimpau* headmen waiting for them at a range of some eight hundred yards. Another two hundred yards beyond lay the Nez Percé encampment. Perry breathed a sigh of relief, the first of the campaign. There weren't enough warriors in that camp to make a real fight of it.

"Officers forward," the command rang down the column.

Captain Boyle held hasty conference. "Theller, take G Company to our right, formed as skirmishers. Perry, take your men to the left in the same manner. I'll be with our guides in the center. We'll form ahead there about three hundred yards. If they want to talk instead of fight, let them come to us."

"Uh, if the captain pleases, sir," David Perry interjected.

"What is it, Lieutenant?"

"Chief Joseph knows me, and trusts me. Perhaps I should be with the party that meets his emissaries?"

"Not necessary, Lieutenant. General Howard is familiar with my methods and will be able to in-

135

stantly evaluate the results we have here today from my report. Well, gentlemen," he dismissed, "shall we get to it?"

How he relished this moment! Ad Chapman licked thick lips and his pale blue eyes twinkled with a light more commonly associated with sexual arousal. He had waited a long time. Now, here, today, he would see his dreams fulfilled. Soon there would be no more of these lice-infested savages to pollute the land. Land that rightfully belonged to civilized whites, like himself. And those horses. How he'd love to have a hundred head or so to start off a nice genteel breeding farm. For the moment he stifled his avarice in order to prime the pump, so to speak.

"Captain, beware of trickery. You can never trust these savages. What may look like a peace banner may turn out to be a war lance piercing your heart."

"Mr. Chapman, I find your animosity consistent, if a bit excessive. This Chief Joseph has not given any sign of hostility in the past. His letters to General Howard, done through an interpreter, were most conciliatory, his arguments well thought out. The general considers him to be a man of intellect, though of somewhat rude quality. Given the advantage of education, one wonders what Joseph might have attained to, actually."

"You're another, ah, advocate for the Indians, Captain? Like Lieutenant Perry?"

"Oh, far from that. And your warning is duly noted. Up ahead there, that knoll. I think that would be a fitting place to hold our parley. If you'd be so kind as to lead the way with your men?"

"As you wish, Captain. At least we'll be prepared in the event of any treachery."

"Ollokot," Joseph called to his brother. "Take the peace banner. Ride with our headmen to meet the soldier chief on the knoll."

Ollokot set aside his other duties and handed Joseph his rifle.

"Here, my brother, I may need this in a hurry, I'd entrust it to no other."

As he did this, the soldiers at the head of the column fanned out to the right side of an officer Joseph did not recognize. Then Lieutenant Perry's men came forward and took position to the left of the knoll. Ollokot glanced at his brother and gestured with his head.

"Do you see him?" he inquired.

Joseph examined the strange officer and a small band of men in regular white man clothes. Beside the officer was a familiar figure, in a large white hat. Ad Chapman. Joseph's lips compressed. Chapman's presence could mean no good for the *Nimpau*. At a nod from Joseph, Ollokot and the peace delegation rode forward.

Slowly the range closed to less than fifty yards. Joseph watched with anxious concern, which turned to horror as, completely without provocation, Chapman raised his rifle and fired into the delegation. Ollokot swayed in his saddle and dropped the peace banner. Anger replaced the numbing shock and Joseph shouted the order to mount and charge.

"You fucking idiot!" Lt. David Perry didn't know if he screamed the words of merely thought them.

Immobile with surprise and shock at this cowardly act of assassination, he could only look on as the

137

Nez Percé warriors flung themselves onto the sides of their swift, spotted-rump horses and, yelling shrilly, charged across the flat, grassy floor of the valley. Perry's quick mind soon saw that even the contingency of treachery by the whites had been planned for, as Ollokot—face grim and bloody from the assassin's bullet—swung his spotted pony around to match stride with that of Joseph. He reached out for the rifle his brother offered him. To Perry's left, the civilians on the knoll, and Captain Boyle, had dismounted and were taking firing positions. Perry had the wit to bark sharp commands.

"Prepare to fire! By the volley . . . Aim! . . . Fire!"

One mighty volley crashed out from the army's right. Through the thinning smoke, Perry quickly realized that the Indians charged straight for the knoll, their fury centered on Ad Chapman's big white hat.

"Wheel left! . . . Aim for the fucking horses. Prepare to fire!" Perry commanded a fraction of a moment too late.'

Rage had not blinded Joseph to the identity of the true enemy. He led his warriors straight toward the white hat that marked the man who had tried to murder his brother. Ollokot, his arm extended, grasped his rifle, which he levered once, before thrusting another fat and shiny .45-60 cartridge through the loading gate. Together they charged the civilians.

"Drive them off that knoll. From there we can set the soldiers to running," Joseph commanded.

"Why has your friend betrayed us?" Ollokot demanded over the tumult of thundering hoofs and crackling firearms.

"It's not Perry. A new soldier and our old enemy, Chapman."

From Joseph's left the rifles of Perry's men barked, then blazed again. Ahead the civilians began to realize that being close to Chapman could be distinctly harmful to their well-being. They began pulling back, to the reverse slope of the knoll. At a yell from Joseph, his warriors opened fire.

"Jeez, they're comin' right at us," a frightened civilian blurted.

A sometimes highwayman and rustler, he had big dreams of a prosperous farm in the Wallowa Valley. Those visions dissolved now in a hail of bullets, the dust, smoke, and the stink of combat. Deep concern for his safety motivated his legs to life and the "local guide" ran for his horse. Not the least to his dismay, he found a number of his fellows similarly engaged.

"Get back here and kill them, damn you!" Ad Chapman bellowed.

Lieutenant Theller's men, afraid to fire lest they down their comrades in arms, fell back and prepared to regroup on more defensible ground. Even had Captain Boyle been with them, or Lieutenant Perry, it is doubtful the maneuver could have met with success. The factor that prevented it was a large column of howling, firing Indians on a level in their center, between each line. Several casualties lay on the low hillock now, and another civilian guide staggered and clutched his breast as he let go the reins of his horse.

It signaled a general retreat.

Retreat became a rout before Joseph's eyes. The

civilians broke entirely and his men swarmed over the knoll. Joseph dismounted and began to shout to his followers to lay down an enfilading fire on the exposed troopers. He spared precious time to send Ollokot on his way.

"Go after them, keep the pressure on with what men you have. I can break the army from here. I know I can. Go with the Spirits, Ollokot."

Half a dozen Nez Percé, then four times that, swiftly growing to a thick clot of busy bronze bodies, covered the hill. With surprising accuracy they poured fire into exposed ranks of the soldiers to either side. Lieutenant Theller received a slight wound and swayed in his saddle. His men's orderly withdrawal became a screaming, jerk-kneed stampede.

Nez Percé bullets snapped around them, adding impetus to their flight. Perry's men knew but little more perseverance. They, too, sought escape from the certain death that cracked by to left and right. Perry felt the pressure and yielded to it.

Now all the soldiers fled the battlefield. What had begun only fleeting seconds before with an assassination attempt ended in ignominious defeat.

Chapter 16

"Thickwoods River ahead," Sergeant Two-Bellies announced, using the Sioux designation rather than the Crow for the North Fork of the Cheyenne River.

Insects hummed in the warm July weather, and birdsong provided a counterpoint to the soughing of the light breeze. Eli Holten studied the distance and nodded.

"There's a bad ford up here as I recall," Eli responded.

"Shortest way," the Crow scout sergeant answered flatly.

Holten studied the afternoon sky and gazed over the prairie beyond the river. "We'll take it easy, camp on this side, and cross in the morning with fresh horses."

"Bear Coat wants us . . ." Two-Bellies started, then cut off at the expression darkening Eli's face.

"No need to lose any men or horses in the effort, Sergeant."

A musing expression crossed the Crow scout's face. "You think much of the men you lead, Tall Bear."

Eli answered him lightly, yet in the proper frame to impress his new ally. "If they all die or are wounded

141

and can't fight, who then can I lead?"

Two-Bellies laughed softly. "You would have made a good Absaroka warrior."

Night camp passed uneventfully. Shortly before sundown, one of the Crows shot a small antelope and they feasted on fresh meat before turning in for a good rest. Again in the morning, the horses were heavily grained at Eli's instruction, and then the crossing had to be faced.

Two of the Crow scouts plunged into the water together, taking along ropes tied together to form a support that spanned the river. The ends were secured to low willow trunks and the others began to cross. Despite the swift current, swollen from recent rains, the detail experienced little difficulty until midstream. There their mounts carried downstream until they bowed the rope deeply. The Crows slipped into the water and held onto the safety line with one hand, while they pulled their horses along with the other. Within fifteen minutes of starting, half of the contingent had made the passage. Then a shot cracked from a low knoll some fifty yards distant.

They had passed Holten's camp in the night. Some of the less intelligent among his band of brigands had complained to Big Foot that they should have attacked then. Get the man responsible for breaking up the squaw ring and the stolen-army-goods racket while he slept, they urged.

"No, they can fight back in their camp," Big Foot had replied in a hissing, whispered argument. "Tomorrow is the time. At the ford."

Now the wisdom of his position dissolved as the first shot blasted the quiet of early morning. The slug from an overeager ambusher's rifle slammed into the point of a Crow scout's left shoulder and pitched him face-first into the water. Struggling feebly, he disappeared as the swift current carried him away. Big Foot's border thugs immediately opened up on the fording column.

Too soon, damn it, too soon! Big Food thought furiously. All he could do now was try to save the situation before it fell apart around them. He took aim and fired a hasty shot at Eli Holten.

To his surprise and discomfort, reaction came at once. Eli Holten's .45–60 Winchester '76 blasted in response. The fat slugs slammed into the hastily arranged dirt embankments that concealed the ambushers, showering Big Foot's eyes with grit. Frightened by the violence of the impacts, one of them rose incautiously into the open. Exactly what the scout wanted, Big Foot knew with clarity, as he dug particles of soil from his eye sockets.

Four hundred and five grains of blunt-nosed lead collided with the frightened hardcase's forehead and exploded the back of his head. Blood, brains, and tissue flew in a gory spray. Two men lurched and made as if to break off the engagement. Big Foot put a bullet close to the feet of one of them.

"Hold your place, damn it," he growled.

The volume of fire from the ambushed Crows increased rapidly. Chips of stone and clumps of turf flew into the air around the bushwhacker's emplacements. Cries of discomfort and alarm grew. Those of the scouts who had not yet crossed remained on the far shore, dismounted, and began to place careful shots that kept down the heads of the would-be assassins. Eli Holten rallied those on the near shore and led them in an impromptu charge.

With wild war cries and rapid fire, the small force assaulted the positions of the ambushers.

Eli Holten silently cursed himself as the sound of the first shot swelled across the ground. For all his caution they had been ambushed anyway. He had his Winchester out of the saddle scabbard and a round chambered before he gave it conscious notice. He sighted slightly to the left of the thinning puff of smoke and squeezed the trigger.

Around him the Crow scouts were doing the same. A solid hail of lead sped toward the hiding places of the enemy. Uttering a faint cry, one of the ambushers rose upward. Eli swung his sights on the man at once and let go a round. With only a fractional pause, the man flipped backward and disappeared in a thin shower of the contents of his head.

"Pin them down!" he shouted to the Crows on the far bank. "You men, come with me," he told those close to him.

Like a single entity, they rose up and advanced on their attackers, firing and shouting ululating war cries. It soon became apparent to everyone that Big Foot had chosen poorly among the riffraff he had brought along. One by one they broke and ran to save their skins. The big, lumbering mixed-blood had no option but to follow.

With a hoot of derisive satisfaction, the victorious scouts sent a few rounds after the fleeing hardcases. Holten held a long bead on Big Foot and squeezed off a shot that slapped through the lat muscle of the 'breed's right side. Then the last of the rabble disappeared over a low swale.

"They won't be back," Holten predicted confidently. "We're getting too close to Miles for that. When the time comes, I want Big Foot all for myself."

Two-Bellies grinned happily. Yes, Tall Bear would have made a *great* Absaroka warrior.

Yapping dogs made the loudest sound in the village Crazy Horse had established along the bank of the Missouri River at the Red Cloud agency. The voices of those not attending the council were muted. Only an occasional child's shrill cry disturbed the somber mood. Unlike the councils of the people, this one was held in one of the white man's buildings, where only the attending chiefs could overhear the proceedings.

"We have been promised our own agency," Crazy Horse declared stubbornly, through Johnny Broughier's interpretation. "Bear Coat Miles told us we would have a place of our own before the leaves turned."

"That's a long way away, Crazy Horse," General George Crook responded. "So far we have heard nothing from Washington. Without the approval of the Great White Father's, ah—er, sub-chiefs, we cannot give you ground that is not ours to give."

"All the ground for many days' ride in any direction belongs to the Lakota. If the Great White Father has not yet decided which small portion we could keep," Crazy Horse paused for emphasis, "why did Bear Coat and Three Stars promise what they couldn't deliver?"

"Ummm. A fair question, Crazy Horse," Crook admitted. "But tell me, about the other matter we discussed this morning? A formerly peaceful, cooperative chief, Chief Joseph of the Nez Percé, has apparently gone on the warpath against General Howard far to the west of us. He, Joseph, is leading his people in a northeasterly direction. If they are not

stopped, it is believed they will come into this territory. General Miles is to be detailed to take to the
field should this occur and he would very much like
to have you and your picked men scout for him."

A distant look washed over Crazy Horse's face.
"You would have us fight against this Chief Joseph?"

"Ah . . . yes. If it came to that."

Crazy Horse presented the others with a growing,
rueful smile. "You have insisted that I put aside the
warpath, which I've done. Now you wish that I *take
up* arms and fight for you. I would have to have time
to think on this matter."

"You can have time, of course. Only not a lot of
it. Each day the situation grows more critical. Already Joseph has crossed Idaho and is approaching
the Yellowstone country. He travels with all his
women and children, his moving lodges, and horse
herds."

That produced a twisted grin on Crazy Horse's
lips. "If that is true, he's not on the warpath," the
Oglala chief stated flatly. "A war party does not
travel with women and children, or with dogs and
many horses to give sign of their passage. You're
wise in these ways, Three Stars. Don't you know this
to be a true thing?"

"I, ah, well, yes. I suppose you're right. But they're
killing white people along their route. They must be
stopped, turned back."

"You would have us, and Bear Coat, make war on
these people?"

Crook only nodded. Crazy Horse rose from his
seated position and crossed his arms over his chest.

"I know of this Man of Magic Thunder. When the
women and children of such a great friend of the
whites as Joseph are not safe from the bullets of your
soldiers, what Indian can be?"

Chagrined at how simply he had been led into this trap by Crazy Horse, General Crook exchanged a sharp glance with Captain Bourke. John G. Bourke made a barely perceptible motion of his head, as though to say, "Didn't I tell you he was crafty and unpredictable?" Crook compressed his lips and labored to frame a reply. He was not a political animal, prided himself on not being so. Yet his natural inclinations made him ill-equipped to deal with the wheels-within-wheels of convoluted Sioux social and political structure.

Apaches were Apaches and nothing more. So were the Utes. They were not family, sept and clan, band and tribe, or warrior and medicine societies, medicine chiefs, civil chiefs and war chiefs. The Sioux confounded him. How *should* he answer Crazy Horse?

"I'm afraid, Crazy Horse, that you read too much into the intentions of the army as regards Chief Joseph," Crook said blandly. "Take time to consider carefully and we will speak of it again in late afternoon." Crook looked to Johnny to interpret.

"it is not your place, Crazy Horse, to question the intentions of the army. Before anything else can be decided, you must make a decision to join us against Chief Joseph before the sun is a hand's breadth above the western horizon," Crazy Horse heard, not in the soft words and gentle phrases of Crook, but in the harsh, commanding tone and insulting terms of Johnny Broughier.

From the first, Crazy Horse had been puzzled that when he spoke the good words and the approval of his head men had been so obvious, Red Cloud and his chiefs looked sly, while Three Stars reacted with growing wrath. It now came to him, with this marked difference in voice tone, that the interpreter exchanged good words for bad ones, twisting both sides of the counciling, so that he and Three Stars came out looking to each other as enemies. A glance at Woman's Dress confirmed this for him, as the army's "tame" Oglala smiled evilly at him. Anger rose and he snapped a final question.

"That was not the stated reason for this council. What about a home for my people?"

"I will not talk of this. I demand a home for my people," Johnny Broughier rendered it.

General Crook flushed with pique. "I have told you, I will do what I can. Meanwhile, I must have your decision on whether you will ride with Miles."

"There can be no thought of it until you agree to fight with Bear Coat," Crazy Horse heard the lying lips declare.

Knowing that what is not spoken cannot be turned against him, Crazy Horse said no more. Eyes flashing obsidian hate at Johnny Broughier, he stalked away from the conference. Behind him, Captain John Bourke and Johnny Broughier bent close to General Crook, each intent upon heaping more mendacious imprecations upon Crazy Horse and his Oglalas.

Chapter 17

Beaming with all the glorious radiance of the first sun of spring, Nelson A. Miles read the contents of one of the dispatches Eli Holten had brought along with him from Fort Thompson. He set the paper aside and clapped the scout on one shoulder.

"By all the Furies, I've got my star back. That's from Headquarters, the War Department. I've been confirmed in the rank of brigadier general. The appointment won't take effect until after this campaign, but at least now I can afford that brandy you've been asking for, Holten."

"Congratulations, General. I gather that it's been a month in getting from them to you. It's good news, all the same."

"The other one isn't, I'm afraid. New orders. And a good thing you got here when you did. First off, tell me of what's going on south of us?"

Eli assessed the situation of Crazy Horse at the Red Cloud agency, which brought a frown of disapproval from Miles. "Damn it, he should have an agency of his own," the newly appointed general summed up.

"I agree. There's some good news, though." Eli told Miles of what went on at the Box M ranch, named Duncan McAllister as the man behind the rustling, and informed Miles that Colonel Clark remained obstinate about immediate arrest of the criminals.

"We'll see about that," Miles growled back.

Next Eli elaborated on the squaw murder ring and its disposition, including the arrest of Burdette and the flight of Big Foot, and the ambush attempt. At the conclusion of the scout's tale, Miles tapped the sheaf of orders.

"These new orders," he began, "are only official confirmation of what I've obtained by telegraph. Chief Joseph and his Nez Percé have made an outbreak. They are leading Howard a merry chase across Idaho, headed toward the Yellowstone country. A number of whites have been killed. From what I've been able to ascertain, they weren't any who didn't deserve it. Border trash for the most part. Some adventurers out to be the ones who 'got' Chief Joseph. But it's put the army in a panic."

"In what way, General?"

"There are massive troop movements everywhere. Why, they've even sent for a brigade of artillery from Alaska. Generals Terry, Cook, and I have been put on orders. That's what this is all about. I'm to break off my pursuit of Gall—which I've already done—and march westward in an attempt to be the army's goalkeeper and prevent Joseph's escape over the Canadian border. Since I've been in the field for months now, my scouts are exhausted. I want to rely on you and the Crows to locate Joseph."

"That should be no problem, General."

"You think not, Holten? I've already mentioned it to their noncom, ah, Two-Bellies, and he's refused flatly. When it comes to Indians fighting Indians, they have that choice, as you know. I want you to try to persuade them to the contrary."

150

"I'll try. Failing that, what alternative is there?"

"A small party of Oglalas showed up a week ago, led by Little Big Man. He's bitter and angry at Crazy Horse for going in to the agency. He said he would fight for us, but never live like a white man in a wooden box."

"Ummmm. He's a good man in a fight. Let me talk to the Crows."

Chief Joseph heard the words of his scout with trepidation. Howard had come across Cottonwood Creek at last. With him he brought his cavalry and the infantry, who were beyond counting. All those men and cannon and the fast-shooting guns. Had he the choice, he would never face them. Yet, what could he do? The council had voted against surrender, and even against his compromise proposal to run for Canada. The voices of the young cried so loudly.

Too-hool-hool-zote, swinging the other chiefs behind him with eloquence, determined to whip Howard in their own homeland. He'd made fine, glowing speeches about how good it would be to die fighting for the country that held the bones of their ancestors. Fools! What would it profit them that the land would now hold *their* bones? Bitterness seeped through Joseph. They would not follow him out of the trap, yet they demanded he lead the resistance. So be it, then.

Here on the Clearwater Joseph would make his stand. Had we the strength then, way back in White Bird canyon, that we have now, he thought sadly. It could have been ended easily. Not with the sixty, who were blamed for stealing livestock from the whites, when in truth, the whites had stolen from each other and laid the blame on the *Nimpau*. But with nearly

151

three hundred, as he now led, that would not have happened. Nor would have peaceful Looking Glass been driven out when the troops came to his town and let the civilians who guided them open fire, wounding Red Heart on the threshold of his farmhouse.

Not with three hundred to drive them away. Hadn't his sixty scattered the soldiers at White Bird when they treacherously let Ad Chapman try to murder Ollokot? Yes, he knew it to be so. Hadn't he won every engagement since, losing so few warriors, while the whites' fallen counted as the stars? Yet he knew his own casualties could never be replaced. And now he must fight again.

Sitting uncomfortably atop his mount in the hot July sun, General Howard fumbled out his pocket watch. Eleven past one, he noted. Trimble and his men had made good time. A seven-mile march on this excellent piece of tableland. Howard felt confident he had the Nez Percé trapped at last. Only narrow ravines and precipitious thousand-foot cliffs gave egress. There in the distance, the general saw a pair of rapidly moving specks. They grew in size, and after a few minutes, Lieutenant Fletcher and Ad Chapman galloped up.

"Indians, sir," the young officer reported. "They're driving some cattle through these coulees."

"Camp can't be far," Chapman put in.

At once Howard had the three artillery pieces that had accompanied him moved into position with a company of infantry at the crest of the bluffs. He now discovered the camp to be to his rear by some distance, on a small flat at the mouth of Cottonwood Creek. He commanded the gunners to be quick about it and get off a few rounds.

All of the balls fell far short. It left no doubt, though, of the presence of soldiers. Almost at once, a small band of warriors, led by Too-hool-hool-zote, raced to the top of the bluff and engaged Howard. His advance stalled, his command split into thirds, and the pack train dangerously exposed, Howard desperately signaled for Lieutenant Trimble to turn about and come to his aid.

Bullets snapped through the air and thudded into the ground. Forced to dig in and fight, Lieutenant Trimble and his men found themselves under attack from two sides. Plunging fire dropped on them from the bluffs as well. In the dust, heat, and confusion men died screaming. Trimble looked around him in growing concern.

"We've got to get through to the rest of the column," he declared.

"Yes, sir," his first sergeant responded. "But they're under fire, too. At least we have some protection from the shelved banks of the creek."

"It might be better if our lines were consolidated here," Trimble speculated aloud. "Signal the others, Sergeant."

"Yes, sir."

Howard's reply, when it came, stunned the young officer. " 'Extend your lines, as is the right flank. That way we can surround them.' Hasn't he any idea?" Trimble groaned.

A good soldier, though, he complied with his commander's orders. Within half an hour Howard's lines were extended for some two and a half miles, in a rough circle around the village, being attacked from within and without. The Nez Percé marksman-

153

ship proved deadly.

One man had his hat shot off three times. A *Nimpau* sniper with a telescopic sight picked off one officer after another until a short, courageous sally brought him down. His frightfully lethal weapon was presented to General Howard, who, with only one arm, would never be able to use it efficiently.

"Many soldiers are dying, "Ollokot observed to his brother.

"Yes," Joseph replied sadly. "For every one of them who falls, two more spring up. For us, each man is a loss we can't replace. We are badly situated here."

"How so? Aren't we on both sides of the enemy?" Ollokot inquired a bit smugly.

"We must be careful, Ollokot, or we can be caught in the middle," Joseph remarked grimly. He pointed to the distant trail. "See there. More soldiers. Pony soldiers and supplies to feed the long-shooting guns." He turned to a pair of trusted headmen. "Ride out with your warriors and try to stop the pony soldiers from joining the others."

Captain James Jackson, at the head of B Company of the First Cavalry, signaled his men to advance in a wedge formation, firing as they rode. Ahead, Captain Miller's hard-pressed command cheered them on and doubled their fire into the Indian defenders' positions. Fast riding Nez Percé warriors, on their spotted-rump ponies, were discovered attempting to turn the flank.

"Form the battalion to the left flank. As skirmishers . . . forward . . . hoooo!"

Caught unaware, the *Nimpau* attempted to turn this new tactic to their advantage, only to fail miserably as Captain Rodney's company outflanked the flankers and began to roll up the Indian line. The mounted charge broke against the wave of cavalry and the Nez Percé began to retreat. For the first time, Joseph saw terrible defeat sweeping down upon him and his people.

Quickly the retreat became a rout. The survivors, along with women, children, and old people, fled down the bluffs to the riverbank. There the headmen, urged on by Joseph, tried to rally their forces. Mothers and wives would have none of it. So precipitously did the flight begin that kettles of meat were left cooking on the fires. Food, clothing, blankets, were abandoned. The *Nimpau* sought escape at the terrible cost of fortunes in ornate beadwork, exquisite saddles, jewelry, and all their possessions, save the precious horse herd.

By three in the afternoon, Brigadier General Oliver Howard stood spread-legged in the center of the village, surveying his enormous victory. While his troops went about caring for the wounded, seeking any hidden warriors, and securing the area for their own safety, the civilians set to searching for abandoned caches of food and valuables. Vulture-like, they amassed huge piles of loot from which they would later profit. Disgusted, Howard was constrained to mutter in anger:

"God strike them for their greed. They've even refused to help bury the dead."

In fear and trembling for the first time, the survivors made their hurried way in a northeasterly direction. Behind them, abandoned with their treasures, lay peace and security. With bitter foreknowledge, Chief Joseph considered what lay ahead for them.

"All faces will be turned against us now," he sadly told his brother. "We are exiles and have become as beggars. No man will succor us."

Chapter 18

Weeks passed with flying skirmishes between Chief Joseph's Nez Percé and the army. The entire nation watched, while locals in the path of his flight panicked. More and more supplies and troops joined Brigadier General Howard's command and the pursuit commenced in earnest once more. Newspapers headlined the news that the *Nimpau* had crossed over into Montana, in the region of the Lolo River. Too late, many citizens realized that this presented a distinct threat to their enjoyment of a visit to the spectacular scenes of the Yellowstone Valley.

Some few hearty souls could not be dissuaded, though ample cause argued for the abandonment of their excursion. The result was almost humorously predictable.

A group of tourists from Raidersburg, Pennsylvania, journeyed out into the awesome valleys and bluffs of Yellowstone, a company of three Concord coaches especially designed for the sightseeing trade. The stages had seats rigged on top and even one overhanging the rear, aptly called the Giddy Bench. For several days, until the twenty-fourth of August, their expedition encountered nothing dangerous, save for a few curious bears.

They decided upon a side excursion along the

Firehole River and made plans for camping at a spot some three miles south of the Gibbon River. On the way westward to their proposed campsite, one of the women caught sight of a large field of berry bushes, the branches heavy-laden with ripe fruit.

"Wouldn't they be marvelous for supper tonight?" she inquired of no one in particular. "Oh, please, driver, stop a while so we can pick a goodly supply."

"Wouldn't want to be out there if a b'ar came along," the grizzled teamster responded. "They take quite a fancy to them berries."

"No old bear is going to amble by right now," the young lady protested. Think of how divine those berries will taste, swimming in cream, or maybe baked into thick, juicy pies?"

The teamster licked his lips and swallowed hard. It had been a long while since he'd enjoyed a good pie. Nodding, he reined in, the other coaches followed his lead. The eager young lady announced the reason for the stop and several like-minded women joined her.

Industriously they worked their way toward a slight swale while the guides fidgeted and glanced around uneasily. A few moments more and the ladies disappeared. One of the teamsters rose on his coach seat and grasped his rifle. Nothing untoward happened for a long while. Then came sounds of fear from beyond the rise.

On the far side of the small rise the delicate blossoms of Eastern propriety came face to face with two dozen of Chief Joseph's Nez Percé warriors. The sudden appearance of the painted savages—though they wore no paint and were merely scouting for the long column of approaching *Nimpau*—completely unnerved the ladies. They turned as one and ran shrieking from the equally astonished Indians.

Squealing with fright, the women hoisted high the

hems of their skirts and petticoats and ran toward the Concord coaches that had brought them here. Gathered berries flew in all directions. The scant protection the others in their sightseeing group could offer meant less than the security they hoped to achieve in numbers.

The fleetest of them had disappeared from view over the rise before the warriors reacted and gave chase. Some of the laggards were scooped up off the ground in a laughing, playful manner.

"We'll take them back to Hienmot," Camas Heart decided for the others.

"There will be more," another brave cautioned.

"Why, then, let's go and get them, too. Are all of you women?" he asked the frightened lady over his lap.

Barbara Ritchie blinked her big, blue eyes and listened uncomprehendingly to the gibberish directed to her. Her face flamed with humiliation at the undignified position she found herself in and she tried to wriggle around to a face-up condition. Her captor barred her movement with a hard forearm.

"You . . . women?" he asked again in broken English.

"N-no," Barbara managed to stammer. "N-n-not all of us. There's men along, with guns. Lots of men, with big guns," inspiration guided her.

"We make fight," the hatchet-faced warrior declared.

"No—no, don't do that. You wouldn't want to do that," she cajoled. "We came to see the pretty rocks and the, ah—ah, magic waters. We want only peace."

"We want peace . . . white soldier take away," came a flat statement.

"Oh, I am sorry . . . "

"You stay . . . us now."

159

"I can't. Don't you see? Ooooh!" Barbara wailed as the brave and those with him wheeled and rode off with their captives.

Things had started looking up for Crazy Horse, though it left him somewhat puzzled. After much meditation, and hearing of the running battle across far country that brought Joseph and his people closer, he had agreed to fight for the army against Joseph. Only a short while ago—the messenger still refreshed himself after galloping to Crazy Horse's camp—he'd received word from Three Stars that he, the general, didn't want help from Crazy Horse. To complicate matters, he had visitors, who brought their own disturbing news.

Colonel Clark sat in the lodge to Crazy Horse's left, beside Big Bat, who served as interpreter. They had been coming frequently of late, a circumstance that also mystified Crazy Horse. Seated to his right, in the place of honor, was faithful Little Hawk. Cetanla could always be counted on to give good advice. So it was that Crazy Horse listened closely when he spoke now in a low tone so that the others did not hear.

"I don't like these two being here. They're close to Three Stars Crook. As you know, I will never approve of him or those close to him. I believe that Three Stars does not trust you. That is why he has now said no, for us not to fight against Joseph. He's afraid of what you might do with the ponies and guns it would take to go to war."

"Little Hawk," Colonel Clark spoke up, interrupting. "I would be interested in your opinion. Crazy Horse admits to being baffled by General Crook's decision. I agree. It's not like him to change his mind so quickly. What do you think?"

Cetanla frowned. Had White Hat some means to look within his head? No matter, truth was truth. "I think that Three Stars suspects Crazy Horse might make common cause with Chief Joseph and flee with him to the Grandmother Land, fighting all the way."

"He's a blunt bastard," Colonel Clark muttered to Big Bat after the translation.

"He's a snake," Big Bat answered with poison tongue. "Like Crazy Horse, he can't be trusted."

Strange Man, as Crazy Horse was sometimes called of late, made soft reply, defending himself. "I've had ample opportunity to go north to where Sitting Bull lives with the Grandmother's people, if I had chosen to do so. I did not. Why should Three Stars think I would now? Besides, I have given my word as a Lakota."

Colonel Clark pondered this, despite Big Bat's acid interpretation. It made sense. Besides, he hurried to point out, "I, too, feel this can't be the case. After all, General Crook has promised the guns and ponies for a fall buffalo hunt. If he thought you'd use them against us then, he'd never have agreed."

"This is good," Crazy Horse decided after a moment's thought. "It will go a long way toward settling the people and building trust. New lodges for a new start. By then we will have our own agency . . . ?" he left the question hanging.

Before Clark could frame an answer, the door flap to the lodge was yanked roughly aside and Johnny Broughier entered, scowling, and without invitation. Well aware of Indian protocol, Colonel Clark showed visible disapproval of this rudeness. Broughier addressed him, rather than the owner of the lodge, another lapse in manners that irritated the white officer.

"You should not be here without an escort, Colonel. Crazy Horse is a dangerous man. He plots against you always."

This had become altogether too much. Colonel Clark understood Big Bat, his mendaciousness toward Crazy Horse based in envy and relatively harmless by being so transparent. Johnny Broughier was another matter. The failure of the quarter-blood scout to back Eli Holten and end the rustling affair still rankled. Accordingly, he twisted his lips into a grimace of distaste.

Laughing coldly, Clark told Broughier, "You're mistaken there, Johnny. I find the chief to be a regular gentlemen, which is more than I can say for you. I hear enough voices raised in niggling, petty complaints against Crazy Horse—*there, that ought to take care of Big Bat, too*—without adding yours to it also. I have an interpreter here already, one who is quite competent. Since I do not need your services and you weren't invited by my host, I suggest you leave before you breach any more Sioux etiquette."

Livid, yet helpless to raise any protest lest he betray his partisanship even further, Johnny backed to the entrance and left the lodge. Clark turned a radiant, sincere smile on Crazy Horse.

"I'm going to ask Big Bat to relate that little exchange to you, Crazy Horse. And then I'm going to add my apologies to you for the man's rudeness."

Yes, Crazy Horse thought when he had heard the words, things had definitely begun to look up.

It wouldn't do for much longer, Eli Holten thought. Over the long weeks since he'd joined Nelson Miles's command, he had been using up his scouts sending negative reports to Miles. Less than

162

an hour ago, the last one, except for Little Big Man, had departed with the less-than-elevating news that no sign had been seen of Chief Joseph and his Nez Percé. His one consolation had to be that the column could not be far behind, elsewise Miles would have returned the scouts for replacements. This reduction in force had another unpleasant aspect.

Eli had felt certain for some time now that he and his Oglala scouts had been stalked, even as he stalked the Nez Percé. Though no indication of this surveillance had come to light, Eli's gut instinct told him to be wary. Particularly for the duration of the day.

He and Little Big Man had split up after the early morning departure of the messenger. That way they could cover more ground, with a rendezvous toward evening to compare notes. It also made each of them decidedly vulnerable.

"Could be I made a bad mistake, Sonny," speculation moved him to confide in his mount.

Holten followed a branch of Snake Creek, which led between increasingly steep banks. Here and there along the edges, aspen, larch, and cottonwood had already changed their colors. Pale yellows, a few bold golden swatches, an occasional smear of orange, had nearly wiped out the uniform pastel green. August had ended in sweltering heat, only to be replaced by an early nip of frost and the violent thunderstorms that continued through most of September. Still the battles seesawed between Chief Joseph and the army, with always the Nez Percé forced to give ground, to flee to find another spot from which to stand off their enemy. What did it accomplish?

Pondering on it, Eli silently covered another mile. A spot between his shoulder blades tingled and the muscles of his neck corded up with tension. That unseen gaze had brushed over him again. Unsettled by it, he decided to stop and have a look at what lay to the west of him.

He ground-reined Sonny and changed to moccasins, in order not to disturb the ground of the steep bank. Winchester in one hand, he slowly began to climb. An arm's length beyond midway, Holten froze, sweat suddenly beading his forehead, at the dry-rustle whir of another familiar enemy. So close at hand that he dared not move forward for a look, Eli sensed the proximity of a huge prairie rattler. With infinite slowness he eased his left hand toward the big belt knife he wore at his waist.

It seemed forever before his fingertips brushed the cold steel of the pommel and worked round the haft. As suddenly as it had begun, the whirring stopped. Senses straining, Eli could visualize the vile creature oozing sinuously into coils, preparing to strike at the intruder in its territory. he slid the knife free. The rattler began another warning chorus. With all the agonizing lethargy of his movement to acquire the blade Eli reversed direction and started upward. he could all but actually see the triangular head, darting tongue, and long swaying body. His nostrils tingled with the sharp, stale cucumber odor of the reptile. There. It would be right there, above him, a bit to the left of his head. His arm reached the desired position.

With all his might, he swung the big bowie. He'd have only one chance. If he missed, he'd be struck on the head a fraction of a second later. A fatal wound that would bring a mercifully swift end. A jar ran though his hand and wrist when the blade contacted the thick, muscular body of the snake. Eli completed his follow-through and glanced upward to see a frighteningly long body hurtle through the air.

It fell heavily to the ground below. Sonny snorted,

stomped, then stomped again. The death throes of the huge rattler lasted for some while. Eli paused to ease his rattled nerves and strained body. Great wet spots had spread at both arm pits. Rivulets ran down his forehead and cheeks. Panting from his great exertion, he sheathed his knife and commenced his upward crawl. Chances were, there would be more of the deadly creatures around. His ordeal hardly prepared him for the sight that revealed itself when Eli cautiously crested the ridge and looked onto the wide plain below.

Horses by the hundreds grazed on the brown grass and nibbled at the changing leaves of sparse trees and bushes. Gray horses, white horses and brown, most with spotted hindquarters. Palouse horses of the Nez Percé. Here and there, Eli's keen eyesight picked out the bronze bodies of youthful herdsmen, their long, braided rawhide lariats slung over their shoulders. They sat at ease, though the presence of weapons for even these small boys spoke clearly of the war that dogged them. Eli gave up counting *Nimpau* ponies at a hundred and eighty and estimated the remaining animals in clumps of twenty-five or so.

No doubt of it. He had located the main herd of Chief Joseph's fleeing tribe. With arduous effort he eased his way back down the enbankment. On his feet at the bottom, he took up Sonny's reins and walked the Big Morgan along the ravine for a good mile before mounting. He'd have to find Little Big Man and quickly.

Eli spent two hours taking a roundabout course to their alternate rendezvous point. He found Little Big Man there, in an agitated state.

"You saw them, too?"

"Yes. It is the Nez Percé. Many of them. Women, children, the old, and the warriors."

"I found their horse herd," Eli responded. "Miles must know and come up quickly. Ride to him, Little Big Man."

"What will you do?"

"Keep track of the Nez Percé and mark my trail. Miles has to get here fast or they'll get away to Canada."

Chapter 19

Colonel Clark sat white-lipped with fury atop his mount. In front of him stood three elders of Spotted Tail's band. They had with them the body of a fourth man. To this they gestured as their spokesman spoke with Clark.

"Red Turtle is dead, killed by the men who stole more of our cattle. Why does the army not do anything about it? Is it because the bad men are whites?"

"That has nothing to do with it, Bites His Horse. We are short-handed. Orders from our chiefs have sent many soldiers to stop Chief Joseph and his warriors. When that fighting is over, we can go after the men responsible."

"There are not many buffalo," Bites His Horse replied. "Even if our hunt is good, there will not be enough food for winter. We need the white man's cows."

"I sympathize with you," Clark allowed. "We can only requisition more cattle and bring them to you."

"What? To have them stolen away, too?"

Infuriated that the rustling had begun again, Colonel Clark regarded the murder of Red Turtle as even more dangerous. The Sioux would take this hard. It might result in a general uprising. Just what he needed with all of the cavalry and most of the infantry out with Miles. He could send to Fort Rawlins, yet he knew that the troops there were on alert to be committed to the determined effort against Joseph.

Which left him with nowhere to turn. His attempt to get Johnny Broughier to cooperate had ended in nothing. Broughier was displaying a cowardice far larger than Clark would have expected. Could it be that he feared Crazy Horse? Clark cleared his throat roughly.

"Bring Red Turtle in to the agency. I'll see that you are not disturbed while you prepare him for burial in the Sioux manner."

"You are kind, White Hat. What we want, though, is for our cattle to be brought back and the bad whites punished."

"I'll . . . ah, see what I can do about it," Clark ended weakly, dreading his equivocation.

Eli Holten's following of the Nez Percé turned into more of a circling of the encampment, while Joseph took full advantage of the excellent grass to put strength back into his horses. During the three days of this endeavor, he had made a rough estimate of their numbers. He'd been surprised to learn that so many remained. It was hard to believe they would be so numerous, after all the reported battles and the wearying running, over such a terrific distance.

There was literally scoured ground left behind. The profusion of horses consumed the grass, hoofs and the feet of the people crumpled anything that remained, and their quest for food denuded the long, wide pathway of wildlife. Eli called to mind a story he had heard in his early years of schooling about the

advance of the horde of Genghis Khan. Its passage
had to be something like this, only on a far grander
scale. That, he decided, would describe the flight of
the Nez Percé to General Corrington when he returned to Fort Rawlins. He reached a spot on high
ground to the north of a large grassy plain on the
west bank of the Snake Creek.

Here, he judged, would be about the place where
the tribe would camp for the night. He dismounted
and examined the area on foot for any sign of
advance scouts. If they hadn't passed by, they soon
would, and he would need a place to conceal himself.
He picked his spot carefully and started back to his
horse.

Some fifty yards distant, Eli glanced up to see
Sonny shaking his head and rippling the dark mane
on his neck. Twice the Morgan stamped his left hoof.
Instantly, Holten disappeared into the tall, brown
grass. What could be making him nervous? Eli considered the possibilities while he snaked around a
circular course that would bring him in close without
being observed. He came within fifteen feet of the
ground-hitched stallion without spotting any enemy.
Winchester at the ready, Holten rose and started
directly toward Sonny.

That maneuver forced Big Foot to make a short
charge from his hiding place behind a large hollow
cottonwood log. Mindful, too, not to attract the
attention of Nez Percé scouts, Big Foot held a tomahawk high in attack position. He swung it with all the
might of his huge, powerful frame. Eli raised the
Winchester to block the blow.

Wood splintered from the forestock and sparks
followed as metal crashed noisily against metal. The
force of Big Foot's smash caused the rifle to dis-
charge. Eli wrenched away and noticed that the

magazine tube had been deeply dented, blocking the feed channel.

"I kill you, Holten, you bastard."

"You'd better make it fast, or the Nez Percé will get us both, Big Foot."

Big Foot lunged and Eli side-stepped, then butt-stroked his opponent in the side of his head. Stunned, Big Foot stumbled on a couple of paces. Eli set himself to deliver a smash to the kidneys only to find Big Foot whirled around and charging again. Holten tried to evade the brute in the same manner, only to be slammed to his right, off his feet, from a blade-flat side stroke of the 'hawk.

Fiery pain blossomed in the scout's chest and he knew one or more ribs had been broken. He scrambled over the ground to gain room, then rose to repel another determined attack. A high shriek of punished steel resounded and Eli's hands went momentarily numb from the impact. He saw a long gouge of raw steel on his rifle barrel. A moment later, as he danced away from the menace of Big Foot's tomahawk, he noticed a sizable nick in the bottom portion of the 'hawk's edge. More wary now, Big Foot began to circle. Holten followed along, considering himself to be in a no-win situation. He could not let go of the rifle, yet if he didn't he'd soon be buzzard meat.

"You fook up my sweet game with the squaws, Holten. Get my frien' arrested by the army."

"You're a murdering ball of slimy shit, Big Foot," Holten panted out. "I'm going to enjoy watching you swing on the gallows."

"I no die on rope, Holten. You die here, I go free."

Eli jumped out of the way of a wild swing and risked a quick glance around. No sign yet of the Nez Percé scouts. For the first time since being attacked, Eli had time to consciously plan his actions. He

170

slowly began to shift his circling, carrying the fight to his opponent. He jabbed with the rifle barrel and sought to force Big Foot to retreat. It worked well enough that the huge 'breed stumbled over a small stump of sagebrush.

Immediately Eli leaped in and smashed downward with the buttstock. He rammed hard into Big Foot's ribs and was rewarded with a solid grunt of pain. Then Big Foot slashed in a horizontal arc and buried his tomahawk in the flesh of Eli's right thigh. He gritted his teeth against the pain and tried to wrench away.

Big Foot came with him. Holten stumbled and gasped at the fiery agony in his leg. His left foot gave out from under him and new splinters of hurt radiated from his ankle. It broke him free of the vicious weapon that Big Foot held and he drove a desperate fist into the giant's face. Unable to retain his upright position, Eli fell and rolled on the uneven ground. Big Foot came after him.

With his waning strength, Eli jabbed the muzzle of his Winchester into Big Foot's groin. The half-breed's eyes went wide and round and he puckered his mouth into a small O and sucked air while involuntary tears formed and rolled down his cheeks. Holten ravaged his testicles again. Big Foot began to double over and Holten bashed the top of his skull with the heavy octagonal rifle barrel. Blood pumped with a steady flow from Eli's thigh. He levered himself upward and drove the curved steel butt-plate of the Winchester down on the back of Big Foot's neck. Bones snapped.

Big Foot splayed out on the hard turf and quivered like a rabbit with a broken spine. He gave one mighty heave, gasped for air, and went still. Using the rifle for a crutch, Eli made his way to Sonny and took his field kit from a saddlebag pouch. He delved within and found some folded white cotton squares. Also small bags of potent Sioux herbs. On one piece of cloth he made a paste of various herbs, then cut away his trouser leg and revealed the deep cut made by Big Foot's 'hawk. He put the poultice between two squares, added another pair atop that, and tightly bound it to his thigh.

It staunched the flow of blood and began to tingle in a way that assured the scout he'd not have to worry about infection for a few hours. He couldn't make much distance, and riding was out of the question. Gritting his teeth to the pain he located Big Foot's horse and arranged a camping scene. Then he led Sonny to the creek, stripped off his saddle and bridle, and slapped the big Morgan on the rump.

"Go back, boy," he urged. "Back to Miles."

He doubted that the animal would understand, but at least he had given the beast a chance and, were the cavalry patrols to spot Sonny, they'd know Holten was in danger. Then Eli crossed the sandy soil and waded into the shallow water. He followed the course up to a high rock ledge. There he left the water and took the ridge back to the general area of Big Foot's corpse.

With the last of his dwindling strength, Eli made it to the large, hollow log and crawled within; he drove his saddle and blanket ahead of him and filled all but a small air space with loose sand and rock at the other outlet. With a painful sigh he surrendered to blackness.

Brigidier General Nelson A. Miles sat in a canvas-backed camp chair and surveyed the thick layer of dust on his boots. Like this entire campaign, he ruminated, it covered everything, and no positive results. Even the wide sweeps being made by Holten and his Oglalas had not brought evidence of the Nez Percé. At least the latest dispatches from Crook's headquarters had been encouraging.

Joseph's Nez Percé apparently weren't bent on mindless slaughter. One account in particular had sparked Miles's humor. A group of visitors to the expressive and spectacular country in the valley of the Yellowstone had been surprised by Joseph's tribe more than a month ago. Several woman, a couple of children, and three men had been taken captive for a short while.

They were released somewhat worn about the edges, with their dignity and peace of mind harmed a great deal more than their persons. With the dramatic flare popular to journalists back east, their exploits had been blown up into a harrowing adventure amid primitive savages in geological splendor. So much for that, the saddle-weary commander thought. There had been others who had not fared so well.

Several detachments of "volunteer militia" had ridden out to stop Joseph. Without exception, they had been ridden over as though no more than a fence of cotton gauze. The few lucky ones escaped with their lives. While the yellow press made banner headlines of their slaughter, the more thoughtful, such as that fellow White, in Kansas, had made Joseph the hero of the piece. Now, inexorably, and God granting, he was being drawn to Joseph. What would it be like to face the man some journalists labeled as a "tactical genius"?

"General?" the adjutant came up saluting. "The patrols are back. No sigh of Holten, no sign of the Nez Percé. Weston's detail came across some sign, not Holten's. Unshod ponies, moving the same direction we're going. Best guess is it isn't any of Joseph's people."

"What would you say, Carl?"

"Well, General, if I was a mind to making wild speculations, I'd say it was that bunch that got away when Mr. Holten broke the murder ring. They got to go somewhere, and where better than to join a band of fugitives headin' for Canada?"

"Your hypothesis interests me. Would Joseph welcome them?"

Carl Thornton considered a long moment. "He'd stretch 'em out in the sun to dry, more'n likely. 'Breeds and border riffraff are what caused Joseph his grief in the first place. That chief of his, Wallitits, done in quite a few at the outset of this, way back in the spring. I'd wager they have quite a surprise waiting if they try to contact Joseph."

"Ummm. Then he might do a bit of our dirty work for us, eh? Good enough. I'm anxious to hear from Holten. Somehow I feel that Joseph is a lot closer than we think." Miles rose and stretched with the grace of a large cat. "Holten told me back in April that we'd have snow by October. If he's right it had better hurry. October is all but here."

"Think we'll have Joseph corralled before then, General?"

"Who can say. For my money, I hope so. He's making fools out of Howard and half the United States Army. Damn, but I can't help admire the man."

174

Chapter 20

Pain and thirst formed a ball of white light inside Eli Holten's head. It throbbed, and with each pulse the world swam. Small world, the inside of a cottonwood log. From beyond it, in the real universe, his dizzy consciousness picked out sounds of some interest. Birds trilled and insects hummed close-by. The wind blew fretfully. Eli satisfied himself that it was daytime. Only which day after his fight with Big Foot?

He had no means of knowing how many days had passed. Had the Nez Percé come? Was he now lying in the midst of their camp? Ears straining, he listened for the sounds of human activity. Relief flooded him after several long minutes in which he heard none. Battling the agony of his wounds, Eli retrieved his canteen and a small bag of jerky. He dined sumptuously upon these and then slipped off into a fretful sleep.

Pattering on the top of the log jerked him awake. The irrythmic drumming grew in volume and violence. Whiteness flared in the small air opening he had left, followed almost immediately by a sizzling sound and an enormous explosion of thunder. Hardly five hundred yards away, Holten's groggy mind informed him. The temperature dropped suddenly and a hard pelting assaulted the wood above Eli. Grumbling in the distance and ear-punishingly loud nearby, the celestial cannonading continued. White balls of ice whizzed by the small slice of sky Eli could see. Bowing to the laws of nature, the thunderstorm moved on as Holten grew drowsy again and lapsed into slumber.

He had made it! Joseph rejoiced at the accomplishment. General Howard and his huge army of retribution lay far behind. Only light skirmishes had marked the passing weeks for some time now. The rain of the previous day would slow them more, the heavy wagons and long-shooting guns would be mired down in the greasy gumbo mud of the prairie. It had allowed his people to find shelter beyond Howard's reach.

Here, safe in the Grandmother land, he could look to a new home. Perhaps even this broad, pleasant gulch. His scouts had located it, responding to the sound of a distant rifle shot. Recollection caused Joseph to frown. That shot implied to him that someone knew of their presence. A body had been found at a campsite and the scouts reported it to him. When his eyes took in this remarkable terrain he almost forgot the difficulties the dead man presented to them. How strongly he wished that the scouts could have made contact with whomever had been involved in the killing. He wanted desperately to declare the innocence of his people in this crime to the Canadian authorities. To have them doubt it, Joseph realized, could cause the tribe to be ejected from the safety they had so ardently sought. Yet, had they the guilty party to surrender, it would put a whole new face on the affair.

176

"We should have moved further north," he told Ollokot on this bright and promising morning. "The valley is long and wide, and the further we might have gone the more certain that Howard could not follow."

Ollokot's lightheartedness had returned after he'd viewed their present campsite. "Look around you, Brother. We have everything we want right here. Those high banks reach far enough to hide our lodges from view from the rest of the plain. Our smoke will dissipate before it reaches the tops. And this wide valley along the creek bed has ample grass. When we must, we can move the herd as needed. We're safe and secure in this place. I say we have run enough."

Joseph's features reflected sober contemplation. "That's true, Ollokot. And, at any rate, many of the women and children can go no further. We'll stay a while, rest, recoup. I want two men to ride to the Canadian authorities at Fort Vancouver to claim the Queen's protection and bring the red-shirt men to see the dead man's camp. This can't be done fast enough. After that gunshot and the body . . . " Joseph broke off and shrugged elloquently.

"Water's up higher'n hay in ever' crick from here to the Cascades, Gen'ral," Liver Eating Johnson informed Miles at the midday halt. "Fords washed out, what roads there are ain't for beans. That was sure one heller of a storm."

"Will you ever bring me *good* news, Johnson?" Miles retorted in a sour tone.

Liver Eater grinned boyishly. "Hell, Gen'ral, that's what I thought I was bringin' you." His report ended, Liver Eating Johnson stomped away to find something to fill his rumbling gut.

Miles opened a plain leather map case and took out the official Army Department chart of the area. He studied it idly a few moments, then summoned his officers. When they gathered, he directed their attention to the lines he had drawn on the map.

"Here we are, gentlemen. And, unless I miss my guess by a great deal, here's where Chief Joseph and his people are located. Thanks to that storm, it's a good two days' march there. Holten reported the horse herd, ah . . . here. It's been four days since then. They've outdistanced Howard's main force by some days. Joseph's people must be tired, the horses exhausted. From our scouting reports, right through this stretch would be an ideal place for them to regain strength for the dash to Canada.

"And rest assured that there can be no other course open to Joseph at this time. We know it, and he must also. Why else the northerly bent to his trail? So then," Miles summed up, "It's up to us to get here, across their line of advance, in time to allow Howard to catch up in their rear. Then we have them. Howard has the artillery and Gatling guns, we have the mobility. Between his anvil and our hammer, we shall smash the Nez Percé and return the remnants to a reservation."

"What about reinforcements, sir?" a youthful captain inquired.

"For Joseph? I sincerely doubt that he has received any. Who would send him fighting men?"

"What about Sitting Bull?" Major Hammond suggested.

"Sitting Bull isn't about to come down out of Canada. Not to aid Joseph or anyone else. He might allow a handful of young bucks to join Joseph, but he's also wise enough to realize any general uprising

178

he might signal would be the end of his welcome in Canada," Miles answered confidently.

"We're all that stands between Joseph and safety," Captain Mason observed as he studied the map.

"Exactly," Miles declared. "The entire success of this campaign rests on us, gentlemen. Howard's made a mess of it. Now it's up to us to save the Army's good name. Tomorrow's marching order will put the Seventh Cavalry out front. It will remain that way until the conflict is resolved. That's all."

"We've been betrayed again!" He Dog growled angrily. "Three Stars has broken his word to us."

"*Ta ta ieiya wo*," Crazy Horse responded. "There will be no hunt because we don't have our own agency as yet. White Hat has told me that this is because Bear Coat is still seeking Joseph. The delays are because Bear Coat can't speak our needs for us to the White Father. When he returns, there will be a hunt and we will have our place."

"I no longer trust the words of White Hat," Little Hawk said flatly. "He speaks with one tongue to us and with another to Red Cloud and the Bad Faces. Does he speak with a third to Three Stars and his fellow whites?"

"What would you have us to do, Cetanla?" Crazy Horse inquired, knowing full well what his loyal friend would say.

"Raise up our people. Fill their spirits and make them brave. Then we will go out to live free as we always did. Three Stars and White Hat can't stop us. Most of their men ride with Bear Coat, we are many and can be strong."

"You speak tempting words, Little Hawk," Crazy Horse agreed. "You're not the only one who wishes we had never come in. This is not a good life, not even the life we were promised. Red Cloud grows old and soft and fat. Yet he's like a snake. His eyes are everywhere. If we made such preparations, he would soon know of them and report it to Three Stars. Then the soldiers and the Lakota police would be here, watching our every move, and it would be they, the Bad Faces, who would hide their mouths and laugh, ride out freely if they wanted and lay all blame at our feet."

He Dog waited for the argument in the lodge to subside. "I agree with my brother Crazy Horse. Red Cloud would know, and soon so would the soldiers. We would never be able to get started in a breakout. Talk of running away to our old lands is exciting, but its like a *slukila*. Great fun for a small boy to take hold of and play with, but not yet ready for the work of a man."

General laughter sounded through the lodge. These healthy, lusty young warriors never tired of coarse humor, such as this comparison of their debate over jumping the reservation to a child's penis. When the chuckles ended, Crazy Horse spoke in a kindly tone.

"Sunkbloka gives up something to laugh at even in the midst of difficulties. There are grains of wisdom in what he says. We must do nothing, not the least thing, that would give the evil tongues of the Bad Faces something to wag about. White Hat still comes to see me, and has lately begun to bring other of Three Stars' men. Even the two-bar, Bourke, has begun to turn a good face to our council. At worst, we have to be patient and wait for Bear Coat's return."

Meadowlarks trilled and a constant skree of jays, thrushes, and robins filled the air over the Snake Creek site chosen by Chief Joseph. He and Ollokot stalked along the high lip of prairie to the northwest of the camp. There men labored to build rifle pits that would cover the camps of White Bird's and Too-hool-hool-zote's bands, located on flat bluffs below the swell of the prairie. They could also serve to break any attack from that direction.

"Why are you going to so much trouble?" Ollokot inquired.

"The body of that murdered man bothers me. We have often been blamed for the crimes of others because we are weak. When the Grandmother's men look at the strength we have here, and then at the dead man's camp, they shall find it easier to believe we are innocent seekers of justice." Joseph smiled enigmatically and continued, "We've been here two days and no one has molested us. That's not to say someone won't, and soon. Howard might ignore the boundary. Or the Canadians may try to drive us away before our plea is heard. We must be ready for any eventuality. The firing pits we've set up on the lower flats, and the rock shelters, will protect us somewhat. I also want riflemen to the south of the camp, spread over the area between those two long tongues, to control the mouth of the coulee."

"I see it now. That would limit the choices an enemy would have. They would be driven into our concentrated fire in places that cut them off from escape by the creek on one side, bluffs on the other. Their attacks would have to fail."

Joseph smiled. "You're learning, Ollokot. You and White Bird and Looking Glass are all starting to think like soldiers. It's what I've made myself do in order to defeat them or get away safely. How do they think? How do they plan? It's hard. It makes my head feel swollen. Yet, we must do it. What if I were to fall first in battle?"

"Don't talk like that. Surely none of us fall now that we're in the Grandmother land."

"This may be true . . . yet something keeps calling to me, urging me to hurry, that the work is not yet done."

"You're a visionary. Be satisfied with what we have for now."

Joseph gazed off over the rolling prairie and the hard lines of his face softened. "Perhaps I shall, Ollokot. Before I do, though, I want orders given that a hundred lodges be struck, that the old people, women, and small children are to move further north, deeper into Canada. That way we shall not have them to worry over if the soldiers come."

"It shall be done, Brother. Then we can put a good face to this place and to each other. I'll say it again, I'm tired of running."

"So am I," Joseph agreed, a note of sadness in his voice.

Chapter 21

Two days of rapid travel brought Miles and his command within an easy ride of the spot he had indicated on the map. The day proved uneventful and Miles ordered night bivouac with the tired expectation of yet another day of fruitless pursuit. Cheyenne and Sioux scouts entered camp shortly before darkness fell.

They brought different and electrifying news. "The Nez Percés are camped in a well-laid-out position along Snake Creek," Yellowstone Kelly translated for Miles. "They are but fourteen to sixteen miles from where we stand now."

Galvanized by this intelligence, Miles ordered reveille for two o'clock the next morning. It would be, he noted with a sudden shock, Sunday, September 30th.

Stars shone brightly in a clear sky, the air chilly enough to make a man's bones ache, when the troops fell out to eat a hasty breakfast and prepare for departure. Noting that the Sioux and Cheyenne scouts had undergone a startling transformation, Miles shuddered involuntarily. All had painted for war. Stripped down for a fight, they waited silently on their favorite war ponies. The ground was frozen and a thin film of ice covered the streams. Excitement filled the ranks. Men muttered and joked, smoked, and drank reverently of the strong Arbuckles coffee, as though it might be the last cup they would savor.

"The order of march for today will be as follows," Major Hammond announced when all was in readiness. "Fifth Infantry (Mounted) will lead off, then the Second Cavalry, with the Seventh in the center, to support, pack train to the rear with a guard of two men from each company. All signals will be by hand and voice until the enemy is sighted. *Boots and Saddles* now and mount your men. Prepare to move out. Good luck, gentlemen, and many God defend the right!"

Lieutenant Maus, Yellowstone Kelly, and a few white and Indian scouts had departed earlier and probed in the Bearpaw Mountains for any sign of another hostile camp or any stragglers from Joseph's column. Miles spared them a brief thought before giving the signal to advance.

The contingent of four hundred mounted men, along with a light Hotchkiss gun and a mountain howitzer, moved out at a trot. Dawn came in its usual cotton-candy pink and bands of vivid yellow. Ice crystals danced high in the air and Miles recalled again Eli Holten's prediction that there would be snow by October.

"I'd give anything for a plate of beans and a chunk of that unchewable corned pork right now," groused one trooper as the hours wore on.

At nine-fifteen, word came back by Sioux scouts that the Nez Percé village was still located on the Snake Creek bottom, now less than five miles ahead. Miles held another hasty officers' call.

"I want the Second Cavalry to take the lead. You'll follow the scouts in and charge through the village.

184

The Seventh will follow the Second as support and charge through in the next wave. The Fifth Infantry, along with its howitzer and the pack train, will remain in reserve."

At once the command rippled down the column, "Forward at the trot . . . Yooo!"

Excitement and tension mounted among the troops. Swiftly the miles melted away. At about two miles due south of the village, already on the flood-plain of Snake Creek, the order went out to come to the gallop. The troops were nearing the foot of a six-mile-long slope that stretched practically unbroken back to the vicinity of the conical peaks behind. Most of the camp remained hidden by the old cut-banks, but the ponies grazing on the open prairie to the west, and the men hurrying to secure them, were in plain sight.

"Lieutenant Baird, my compliments to Captain Tyler of the Fifth, and would he incline his troops to the left, follow the Indian scouts who headed for those horses, and attempt to capture the herd from the hostiles," Nelson Miles ordered.

"Yes, sir," Baird responded and galloped off.

"Captain Hale!" Miles called, "Take K Company and make a long sweep of our right flank, try for firing positions on an elevation above the camp."

Miles watched K shear off, satisfied he'd covered the final contingency, allowing the pounding excitement of the gallop to regulate his heartbeat for the demands of the imminent battle. As his pulse thundered to the rhythm of thousands of hooves, echoing eerily on the frozen ground, a crazy phrase kept worming through his consciousness. "The wings of eagles."

"What the . . . " Miles drew sudden rein, "Halt the column!"

Ahead the earth fell away abruptly.

A devastating, ripping crash drew Miles attention to the right where K Company's van thrashed helplessly in a tangle of men and horses. Directly ahead of them a great cloud of white smoke abruptly showed winks of red fire, and more of Hale's command collapsed. Men began to bail off their horses, some with the presence of mind to turn the animals side-on, into the deadly hail.

Through this shock, Miles saw one trooper in the rear spur his mount from the field, and was strangely cheered to see him throw up his hands and tumble backward over the rump of the plunging animal. In seconds, K Company was reduced from a gallant charge to men clawing the earth and cowering behind fallen horses and even the bodies of comrades. Miles raised his hand to order a supporting charge when he realized he'd ridden out onto a long point of high ground and was now surrounded by a sheer drop of some forty feet.

"Captain Moylan!" Miles saw the trumpeter double up, realizing he was also taking fire. "Dismount the men except for horse holders and lead them to the relief of K Company."

Damn, what the hell was he doing playing soldier? From now on he was going to have to earn his pay as a general, if it wasn't already too late.

"And, Captain," Miles called to his subordinate. "I'll send relief at once."

Joseph scowled into the morning sun at his horse herd. He sat a white mare, dappled by the blue-ringed black spots of a perfect Leopard Palouse. She stamped impatiently, then arched her neck and began to crowd the Spanish bit, impatient at inactivity in

186

the crisp air.

"Damn Howard. There aren't a third of the colts romping and pestering at the mares' sides that there should be. Perhaps I should have led the people here sooner, before the man made me drown women, children, and foals in the floods of the Snake." Joseph sighed, knowing it had not been possible, for no one would have followed. In this daughter of his, he had a listener who was guaranteed to be sympathetic.

"You are sad, my father?"

Joseph shifted his weight in the tooled Mexican stock saddle and smiled down at his fourteen-year-old daughter, the delight of his life, and his heart swelled at the ease with which she controlled her dancing pony.

"At times, Star Daughter, the pipe of a leader grows burdensome beyond understanding."

"My father finds no burden too heavy."

"Knowing you are safe with the other women and children will ease my path."

"Otherwise I would make a great noise. Perhaps I would not even speak to you for making me go with the others."

"Waugh! You have been raised better than that." Belatedly Joseph realized she was teasing, and his features softened. "This place has a bad feel to it now. The morning breeze carries the stink of death from that dead one, and I would have the helpless ones further from the soldiers."

"Your family has been ready since sunrise, Father, were it not for laziness of others, we would be far from . . ."

A rippling thunder of volley fire interrupted, as loaded pack ponies spilled up over the rim of the gulch, travois bouncing along behind. They were driven by screaming squaws and frightened children with sixty picked warriors guarding their rear.

"Soldiers! American soldiers coming!"

Again the crash of rifles.

"Ride, Star Daughter, stay with the women!"

Joseph spun his magnificient Leopard Palouse and charged toward the sound of gunfire.

Sliding his horse down the embankment, Joseph was relieved to see there were no soldiers actually in the camps. Most of the tipis had been packed on the travois, though others were left half dismantled. The firing up on the flats had become general now, the volleys spread out as individuals on both sides took targets of opportunity.

Had the bed of Snake Creek run bank to bank, the camps of the four bands under Joseph would have occupied three large islands. Joseph thundered north, skirted slightly to the west of his band's camp on the first island, then flashed past the encampments of Looking Glass and White Bird on the second.

Tool-hool-hool-zote's band occupied the third island and had built an elaborate rock fortification that Joseph intended to use as his command post. A ricochet moaned past and thunked into the far bank as he slid his mare to a stop behind the rocks.

"Lean Elk!" Joseph pointed even as he swung from the saddle, "Take five good shots and fort up on the north side of that point. Where is Tool-hool-hool-zote?"

Lean Elk, whom the whites had dubbed Poker Joe for the impassiveness of his countenance, pointed north.

"Cavalry chase women, him take two hands warriors to make ambush."

"Waugh! I need someone to lead . . . Ah, White

Bird, take as many men as you can gather and slip down the long gully to the south and east. Once you are behind the soldiers our men have pinned down on the flats, crawl up behind them and dig in." Joseph paused, to be sure he was understood. "They will try to reinforce those men and reach a position to fire down on the village. You must prevent this."

Captain Owen Hale reveled in his position. Not since he had been a green ensign in the Civil War had he led an independent cavalry force into combat. The blood coursing through his veins to the thunder of hooves did not blind him to the fact that he was leading his men down a long peninsula between two steep-sided gullies. Wisps of blue smoke rose in the morning air ahead, and Hale wondered if there was a way for his troops to ride down into the village he was now certain lay hidden there.

Damn! He may have to take firing positions at the crest and forego the thrill of a charge through the tipis . . .

Like evil white mushrooms, the ground ahead sprouted balls of pale smoke from fiery bases. Something huge and unseen smashed into his mount's breast and the animal collapsed in full stride. Hale heard the air expelled from his horse's lungs, even as he passed over its head to have the wind driven from him by the unyielding earth.

Gasping for breath, Hale fought his way to his knees, stark witness to a frozen tableau. His second-in-command, Lieutenant John Biddle, spurred toward his captain, arm extended for a flying pickup. Men and horses were thrashing in an incredible amount of gore all around him, while a scarlet-splashed guidon bearer fought to keep the flag and himself upright on a horse that was down on its knee's and blowing a veritable fountain of blood from distended nostrils.

Sound suddenly added an extra dimension and Hale seemed to hear an echo of gunfire as background to screaming horses and men. Hooves shook the earth and Hale's heart expanded as he got his feet under him and reached out for Biddle's wrist. From the corner of his eye he saw the guidon bearer lurch backward. In the same instant Biddle's horse grew a blue hole in the center of its forehead blaze. Biddle's right arm seemed to separate at the shoulder and flop wildly outward as three other clearly defined bullet strikes impacted across his chest, blowing the young officer back across his animal's rump.

A great gout of hot blood splashed Hale's face, projected from the nostrils of the dead horse. An instant before the huge carcass struck, Hale's head exploded the impact of five hundred grains of lead.

He would have been gratified to know that his body became part of the breastworks that preserved the lives of a portion of his command.

Long, slanting bars of orange light lingered on the high prairie around the grim valley of Snake Creek. Through the dust, powder smoke, and confusion, a certain calm order began to exert itself. Shortly after noon, Nelson Miles had removed himself from the proximity of the Seventh Cavalry and set up a headquarters tent near the hospital facility. Dozens of men streamed in and out of the surgery. The groans, curses, and cries of the wounded kept a constant pressure on the commander as he sat wearily in his camp chair and surveyed the reports of his field officers.

Love of God! If he could believe the figures, he had lost twenty percent of his command in the first half hour of the battle. Another twelve before the end of this first bloody day of fighting. Better than half of the Nez Percé horse herd had been captured, if that was any consolation, and the Indians must have lost a good fifty or sixty warriors. Compared to ninety-five killed and over a hundred sixty wounded, such numbers became meaningless. Worse, Joseph showed no signs of surrender or even of wanting to parley. Weary of the conflict, Miles ran a hand down his face in an attempt to ease away the numbness.

Many "victories" like this could soon leave a man without any soldiers to command.

Chapter 22

Gagging over the vile stench of putrefaction, Eli
Holten watched the rotten, maggot-infested flesh
slough from his agonized body. An echoing scream
drew his spirit upward in a wild rush, to where his
heartbeat thundered with a monotonous languor. He
tried to lurch upward and banged his head, pain
from the broken ribs driving the breath from his
lungs. He lay back panting in fear and revulsion at
what he perceived as the corruption of his body.
Slowly, his right hand began a cautious exploration
of the aching thigh, ready to jerk back at the first
touch of anything cold and squirmy.

The wound was hot and sore, and the message
from his fingers confused him until he recalled both
where he was and the body of Big Foot, which must
be the source of the hideous stench. Drums! Drums
seeking power, they had melded with his pulsebeat
and brought him out of the coma. Memory of the
Nez Percé penetrated his consciousness, and his gratitude to the unknown drummer became tempered by
the knowledge that he lay very close to an encampment of hostiles.

Eli pulled his bandanna over his mouth and tried breathing through it as he analyzed his position. From what his nostrils told him, he'd been out for several days. He reached, fumbling, for his airhole and punched through the snow that covered it. Bright starlight relieved him of another niggling fear: he definitely was *not* blind, though the effluvium of Big Foot convinced him that his stay here was just as definitely *over*.

The scout forced his way through the barrier he'd placed in the log with the full knowledge that no Indian would willingly expose himself to the nauseating stench of the body.

Once his head cleared the snow-sodden log, Eli picked up the sound of lesser drums that stirred a faint recollection of pounding hoofs, rifle and cannon fire, and the screams of dying men. A battle, or more than one, had been fought while he lay here. The pain in his thigh and a terrible thirst assailed him. Agony seared through him as he dragged himself free of the log. His leg throbbed as he reversed himself and went shoulder deep into the hollow cottonwood to retrieve his rifle, canteen, and medicine bag. Next he removed the bandage and examined his wound by starlight, a feeble instrument at best.

Hot to the touch, the lips of the cut looked black in the inadequate illumination. The poultice had retarded infection, but not entirely prevented it. Eli estimated the sound of the drums originated at a point about a hundred and fifty to two hundred yards downstream. It reminded him of his danger. Not only possible capture waited him, he could also still contract gangrene in the wound. Fortunately, the swelling and pain had diminished to an occasional twinge in his left ankle. Careful of his injury, Eli dragged himself to the water's edge.

Ice shattered musically as he punched open a hole to get to the liquid below. His hand ached from the cold. Ignoring it, he moistened a square of cloth and brought it out into the light. He made a fresh poultice and bandaged the cut. Now was the time for planning.

He rejected several alternatives and at last decided to work his way upstream, away from the hostile camp. According to the stars he had most of the night to do it and an unknown distance to cover. He'd been in worse situations, he assured himself, only damned if he could recall one. Forced to abandon his saddle and other gear, Eli used his Winchester to aid his clumsy movement.

Progress went slowly. Memory proved a tricky guide, with only snatches of lucid consciousness coming forth. Eli felt certain he had not been in the confines of the camp, yet as he made his difficult way along Snake Creek he heard from time to time the liquid syllables that must be the Nez Percé tongue. They seemed to have some sort of fortifications all along the creek. Surely Joseph realized they were still in the United States, Eli pondered. The frigid night held his muscles in a state of quaking rigor. A white plume of vapor formed at his mouth and nostrils. If he didn't find a way out of this soon, Eli knew, he'd freeze.

At last he came to a point opposite a dark, steep bank he estimated to be some forty feet in height. Picking his way carefully, Eli started upward. He'd covered some fifteen feet, hand over hand, when the soft earth gave way under his grasp. His other hand, holding the Winchester, gave no aid and he slid downward. Too late he recalled a slight protuberance he had worked his way over a short while ago. Excrutiating agony lanced through him when his weight came down on his right leg. Holten tasted blood as he bit his lip to prevent a howl of pain. At least, he realized a second later, his descent had ended.

"D'you hear that?" a voice above him asked in English.

How welcome the sound!

"Naw. Keep yer head down. Them damn Injuns can see in the dark. Pop you 'fer yuh said boo."

Slowly, teeth clenched and breath raspy in his throat, Eli started upward again. He eased past the loose soil and grabbed a hackberry bush for better leverage. At last he eased his head over the rim. Less than two feet away he saw the muzzle of a Springfield rifle.

"Don't use that thing, I'm a white man," Holten spoke in a slow, deliberate manner.

"What th' hell!" the picket exploded. "Bart, I got me one over here."

"I'm Eli Holten, the scout. What outfit are you with?"

"Fifth Infantry battalion," came the answer. "Someone said you got killed by the Injuns."

"I will be if you don't help me up on top. My arms are playing out."

"Bart, come here."

"Sure, Jim. Is it really the scout?"

"Yes, goddamn it, I am. Stop asking about it and haul me up."

Strong arms raised the scout to the top of the bluff. He swayed drunkenly and bit back another surge of pain. The two outpost sentries gaped at him in consternation."

"You're hurt. We better get you back to the hospital tent," Jim suggested.

"You take him," Bart declared. "I'll keep a lookout

for both of us."

An endless, fifteen-minute stagger brought Eli to the surgical tent. Two long lines of men, some on cots, others standing, waited to enter the lighted operating room. Everywhere men showed bloody bandages, smashed limbs, cuts, and gouges. One man had his ear shot away, another had a neat hole through both cheeks. Eli waited his turn, enduring as did the others. At last his time came.

The doctor swiftly removed the bandage, scowled at the pungent odor of herbs, and called for a basin of water, his scalpel, and some suturing material.

"It's a wonder that thing didn't rot right off of you. Those stinkin' weeds . . ."

"Those 'stinkin' weeds' as you call them saved my life, Doctor," Eli told him coldly.

"Were you in the fighting at all?"

"No. I had a run-in with Big Foot. That must have been one or two days before Miles got here. I've been in a hollow cottonwood log for, ah . . . How long have you been here?"

"Uh, four, no five days. I've been busy day and night with the wounded. Those damned Nez Percé are fantastic shots."

He went on to complain about field medical conditions, the number of wounded, and the lack of understanding on the part of troop commanders, but Eli didn't hear him. His mind went numb at mention of five days. That would have to mean his fight with Big Foot had taken place nearly a week ago. When the doctor ran down, Holten told him that.

"You don't mean to sit there and tell me you've not had proper medical treatment for seven days? Hell, man, you'd have been dead long ago."

"That's what I mean about those medicine herbs you insulted so freely, Doctor. I learned which ones

196

to gather from a Sioux medicine man and they *do* work. That's the third poultice I've put on during that time. I kept slipping off into sleep, or unconsciousness, and had no idea how long I'd been laid up. How has the fighting gone?"

Doctor Barnes swung his arm around the cot-crowded tent. "See for yourself. The first day we damned near lost it. Got the Second and Seventh Cav shot to doll rags. This Joseph seems to have forgot more about fighting than most commanders'll ever know. Our present leader excepted.

"If it hadn't been for Nelson Miles, we'd be bloated corpses on the prairie and Joseph would be in Canada. Fortunately Howard and the van of his command arrived. His artillery and supply train is less than half a day's ride away now and coming up fast. The general and his staff came in yesterday, along toward dark. Tomorrow should see an end to it."

"So far, Chief Joseph has beaten Howard every time. What suggests this will be otherwise?"

"He's only managed to fight Miles to a standstill, and his losses are great to have done that."

"Joseph could still slip away in the night. He's done it before."

"Yes. But not with his pony herd captured. They're on foot now and determined fighters. I'm afraid it'll get a lot worse before the battle is done. Now, I'll suture this up some, we'll get it bandaged, and then I want you to rest. Also get some food down you. You look like something the cat spit up."

"You're too kind, Doctor. Where can I find Miles?"

"The general's in his headquarters. He's been negotiating since Monday with Joseph for surrender. There's no agreement on terms as yet, but the fighting has slackened off. From what I understand, Joseph's brother has been killed. Also a number of important headmen."

Eli found Miles in his headquarters tent, huddled over a camp stove. The general gestured to a bottle on the table as Holten seated himself. "Might as well help me finish this before Teetotaling Ollie gets here."

"Thank you, General. I can use a good shot. Do you think Joseph will surrender?"

"I don't know. I think he will . . . but then, his enmity toward Howard is enormous. He tells me that three times he attempted to surrender to Howard and that he was refused and fired upon. He thinks Howard is determined to see him dead."

"Do you believe that, General?"

For a moment Miles looked agitated. "Howard is a . . . man of strong opinions. An abstainer, he neither smokes nor drinks. He's small of stature and sensitive about the loss of his arm."

"The sort of man who might carry grudges?"

"I don't know him personally," Miles evaded. "I wouldn't want to judge. When he came in last night, I expected him to seize command as he did with Sturgis. He informed me that he 'had no desire to assume immediate command of the field.' He was friendly enough, and together we laid plans for combining our forces in the event the siege dragged out or if the Sioux came in. He encouraged me in my efforts to win a surrender."

"Then I suppose the only thing is to wait and see. What Joseph will do, what Howard will do, everything." Eli helped himself to more of Miles's whiskey. It would numb the pain better than the laudanum the doctor had given him, which he had not taken. "I don't mean that you should be a fence sitter, General. That's not your way and it's not my intent. What it

198

boils down to is that this whole thing is up to Joseph."

Chief Joseph sat and stared into the low flames of the fire in his lodge. In his mind, images of all those who had died flowed like a river of pain. He saw them clearly. Grieved for them all. Longed to have them back again. Yes, even the soldiers they had killed.

"Each man fights for what he believes in, accepting it as the right," Joseph said aloud.

His wife touched his arm timidly. "Your heavy heart is unlike you, beloved. It is not you who has failed, it's all of us. We should have continued to move on, to reach the Grandmother land for certain before stopping to look back at those who pursued us."

"Yes. It was the worst blow when my messengers returned at the end of the first day's fight and said the red-coat soldiers stopped at a mound of stones and said that it was the sign to show where Canada began. We have forty-seven of the white man's miles to go to that spot. None will make it now, for the soldiers are all over."

"The Teton Sioux, who have been our friends, should have come to our aid," his woman remarked sternly.

"Don't judge them for not throwing away their lives as well."

"What shall you do?"

"Tomorrow we will fight again, convince them it is wise to treat fairly with us. Then we will see."

Eli Holten awakened to the sound of gunfire. He

had rewound and set his watch, and the big Ingersol turnip indicated the hour to be six-thirty. Ricochets howled and moaned through the air and cooks flinched as they went about their open-air preparations for breakfast. Holten found some coffee. It tasted like ambrosia after the previous night, though it emphasized the ravenings of a hunger he'd been unable to fully satisfy earlier. He and Nelson Miles had managed to exterminate the whiskey before Howard returned to the tent. Holten met the now-famous one-armed general and then had departed to find some food and sleep through the night. Now the volume of fire increased from the American positions while Eli sipped the strong, black brew. It told him that Howard's reinforcements had arrived and been put right into the fray.

Using the crutches provided by the doctor, Eli hobbled his way across the encampment to a position where he could watch the fighting. The Indians, he saw at once, had dug in well. From their sheltered firing pits they directed withering volleys and masterful single shots toward any developing threat. Holten's stomach felt distended. He'd consumed six pieces of thick bacon, two pork chops, five flapjacks, and three large cups of coffee. With what he had consumed the night before, he felt like it should fortify him for a while. An early discovery drew his wonder and close observation.

Unlike their brothers of the plains, the Nez Percé rarely exposed themselves to enemy fire. Their low, covered pits and rock fortifications made the hillsides appear as one large wall of loopholes. The soldiers, by contrast, had little shelter, save what they hastily threw up as the fighting wore on. The resulting losses for the army were appalling. While Eli observed and made mental notes, the firing dwindled and ceased altogether. Puffs of powder smoke drifted away on the chill, biting air.

Eli pulled out his watch and noted the time as eight o'clock. The morning had hardly begun. Off to his left he saw some Indians, along with the short, unmistakable, one-armed figure of General Howard, ride toward the hostiles' camp. Curious, Eli made his way over to Miles's headquarters tent.

"Surrender parley," Miles informed him. "Joseph sent word he wanted to talk with Howard."

Together they waited. After a long delay, Howard and the Indians returned. Howard spoke carefully. "Joseph said he had heard your terms and liked them. He asked me mine. I, ah, naturally, deferred to you, sir. He seems distracted somehow. He stares at far-off places. Asked me if I knew where his daughter was, had she been killed."

"Asked the same of me," Miles remarked. "I think it's important to his state of mind. If we knew for certain, could produce the girl, perhaps that would turn his mind."

"Why don't we make provision for a search to recover her in the surrender terms?" Howard suggested.

"Good idea, General," Miles agreed.

Again the treaty party departed. Eli returned to the hospital to have the dressing changed. The doctor marveled at how neatly and swiftly the wound was closing. "You'll be good as new in another week at this rate. Now, if you'd let me tape your ribs . . ."

"I've had broken ribs before. They hurt a hell of a lot more when I had them taped."

"Ummmph! Young whippersnapper and his Indian medicine," the surgeon complained as he walked to a small wood cabinet and withdrew a bottle. "Keep taking the laudanum pills," he instructed, "as needed to lower pain."

"I'd rather have brandy," Eli responded.

Surprisingly the medico winked. "Good idea, young man. These things grow on a person." He gestured with the laudanum pills. "Some can never quit. I don't have any brandy, but there's some powerful Jamaican rum in here for medicinal purposes. Might even join you, if you don't mind."

Eli didn't. Afterward he helped himself to a large dinner of beef, cabbage, onions, and fresh bread. Shortly after two-thirty in the afternoon, Howard and his interpreters returned. Holten hurried to the headquarters tent.

"It's over," Howard announced. "The Nez Percé will surrender beginning now. Chief Joseph and his headmen will give themselves up a little before sundown." He gestured to two Nez Percé herders who had come with him. "They have Joseph's formal reply."

Carefully, Lt. C.E.S. Wood, acting aide-de-camp and acting adjutant general for Miles, took down the reply as the herders delivered it.

"Tell General Howard I know his heart. What he told me before I have in my heart. I am tired of fighting. Looking Glass is dead, Too-hool-hool-zote is dead. The old men are all dead. It is the young men who say yes or no. He who led on the young men is dead. It is cold and we have no blankets. The little children are freezing to death. My people, some of them, have run away to the hills, and have no blankets, no food; no one knows where they are — perhaps freezing to death. I want to have time to look for my children and see how many of them I can find. Maybe I shall find them among the dead. Hear me, my chiefs. I am tired; my heart is sick and sad. From where the sun now stands I will fight no more forever."

A long silence held, broken at last by Nelson Miles. "Thank God. I—I somehow feel so sorry for that poor, broken man."

Chapter 23

As the sun dropped to the level of the prairie and tinged the tawny and white land with waves of ruddy light, Joseph came slowly up the hill. He rode a black pony with a Mexican saddle, and was dressed in a woollen shirt of dark slate color, with a blanket of red, yellow, and blue stripes around his hips, a pair of beadless moccasins on his feet. His front hair had been tied straight back from his forehead with a small strip of otter skin, forming a topknot. The hair at the sides he had braided, and was held back, with the loose locks waving behind, by longer pieces of the same fur. Five of his followers walked beside him, Eli Holten observed.

He remained in the center of the group, the only one on horseback. Joseph had crossed his hands on the pommel of the saddle, his head bowed upon his chest. His warriors talked in eager murmurs, he listened, but made no reply. Behind, the Nez Percé camp lay in lengthening shadows as the little group came up from the darkening valley into the higher light which showed their wretchedness. Joseph rode directly to General Howard, lifting his head, and, with an impulsive gesture, straightened his arm toward the general, offering his rifle in symbolic surrender.

Only Joseph's fine and sensitive face registered the agony this gesture brought him, Eli saw, as though he left his ambition, hope, and all manly endeavors, along with his heart down with his people in the dark valley where the shadows of their defeat were knitting about them a dusky shroud. The tableau held a moment, then Howard motioned Joseph to Miles, who took the rifle as a token of submission. Immediately, the Nez Percé appeared from everywhere, coming forth peacefully to lay down their arms.

It's over, Eli Holten thought, and was surprised to feel the sting of salt water in his eyes. Slowly he hobbled away. His course took him toward the pack train and wagon yard. Over the heads of many mules and horses, he spotted a familiar black neck and wedged head. His gloom instantly dispelled.

"Sonny!" he called out.

The Morgan stallion whickered and tossed its big head. Eli nearly dropped his crutches in his haste to be reunited with his much-loved horse. In a shuffling, jerking gait, he closed the distance and put out a hand. Sonny nuzzled his palm. From behind, a voice spoke that made the reunion even more perfect.

"I recognized him when we pulled in two days ago. General Miles agreed with me we should save Sonny for you in c-case y-y-you c-c-c-came back," Jenny stammered out, tears forming and running unnoticed down her cheeks. "Oh, Eli, I was afraid you wouldn't."

Then they were in each other's arms, hugging and kissing and shaking with the intensity of their emotion.

"When does a man *refuse* an invitation to a feast?" Crazy Horse asked the wind angrily.

He stood before his tipi, wrapped in a heavy buffalo robe, and stared out over the bleak land of the Red Cloud agency. A light dusting of snow turned the vista to a dappled plain of gray, buff, and white. Bowed under the weight of icy crystals, the grass had a forlorn look. Even the wide Missouri had thin skeins of ice stretched out from each bank. It was a time of hibernation and death.

"Do you want an answer to that, old friend?" Little Hawk inquired as he walked up, a big plume of vapor masking his face. "What a morning this is."

"On a morning like this, a man should be able to sleep late, with his woman at his side," Crazy Horse responded. "Instead, I find myself greeting our Father the sun through little holes in a lead-belly sky. Red Cloud refuses to come to our feast-council."

"Of course. It's the council part he wants to avoid." Little Hawk declared. "Look at it from his point of view. This is his home. It should be he who calls for a council. I'd bet my five best horses that he's ready enough to stuff himself at someone else's expense. It's just that he feels a threat to his authority if he acknowledges you to be able to call a council."

"I . . . I never thought of it that way." Crazy Horse's face softened. "Am I the one who's being rude? Am I the insulter and he the offended party?"

Little Hawk put a hand on his shoulder. "Not many of us think so. Red Cloud is an old man. And a dangerous one because he's jealous of his power. If we had an agency of our own . . ."

" '*If we had*, if we had.' I'm tired of hearing that phrase. Winter comes too soon this year. My woman has not yet visited her people at Spotted Tail's village and she continues to weaken every day. She needs the warm, dry air of summer. The white medicine does little good when she is cold to her bones all the time.

She is near the end of her ability to function as a wife."

"How is that?" Little Hawk inquired, disturbed by this news.

"Some days she lacks even the strength to kindle the morning fire, let alone prepare breakfast, or do any of her womanly chores. She lays in her sleeping robes and coughs feebly. Her skin has a pallor and there's a blueness to her lips. What can we do, Cetanla? What can we do to make it all right?"

"Only wait. Little Big Man brings news that Bear Coat has conquered Joseph and is on his way back here. We must wait for Bear Coat."

Huge wagon wheels crunched and ground monotonously over the frozen earth. Jenny Blanchard's new tandem rig Conestoga had all the comfort of being dragged behind a horse, Eli Holten thought as he lay on the pallet atop the load of supplies she hauled. Jenny rode the spring seat she'd had installed, and Marty straddled the broad back of the swing wheeler, chattering incessantly in his newly acquired English and cursing the draft horses exuberantly. Jenny made frequent trips to the interior of the wagon box to check on her patient. Her visits made the time pass much more pleasantly.

Eyes twinkling with mischief, she'd tweak his flaccid member and ask sweetly, "Ready for more tender, loving care?"

For the first few days of the journey she had not elicited any response. The spirit might be willing, as Eli explained to her, but the flesh had taken one hell of a beating. His exhaustion and physical debility made any sort of performance impossible. Yet the scout mended quickly. His body had always had that facility. On the fourth day out, Jenny's overtures were met with a ready and eager reaction.

"Oh! Oh, my lookie here," she chortled with glee when the object of her attention began to rise to its fullness. "I think you're going to live after all."

"How could it be otherwise?" Eli asked teasingly. "You're such a thorough and considerate nurse."

A little nursing was exactly what Jenny had in mind as she bent her head low over his pulsing organ and flicked her tongue lightly across the burning tip. "Wait till tonight," she murmured in the moment before she closed her lips over his silken flesh and commenced to suction Eli into sweet forgetfulness.

That night, and all the rest on the long trail to Fort Benton, became timeless bliss for Eli and Jenny. Only a few twinges of discomfort came from the leg wound, and for a week Eli had been riding Sonny four hours a day when the buildings of Fort Benton came into view.

Once there, Eli bid Jenny a long, loving, and passionate good-bye and set off, under orders, to report to Nelson Miles in the newly completed Fort Keogh. Eli's heart grew heavy as he contemplated each mile that would separate them. Reason told him they would probably not meet again. At least not for a long while. In compensation for that, he made their last night together a splendrous feast of love-making that left them both breathless and weak in their knees. Jenny cried. She, too, sensed this was a final parting. Marty Richter manfully fought back tears the next morning and solemnly shook Eli's hand. Then he jumped up on Sonny's left stirrup and gave the scout a powerful hug and a tender kiss on his cheek.

Eli swallowed the lump in his throat and rode out, bound for Keogh.

"I tell you this is a true thing. *Hooitu yolo!*" Little Hawk repeated himself for emphasis. "Woman's Dress and Johnny Broughier have twisted White Hat's thinking. The Indian police are even now planning for a raiding party. They will lead a number of Red Cloud's loafers against our village. White Hat thinks it is to look for hidden guns. They want to start a fight and blame it on you, so that they can arrest you."

"How can they? If we don't fight, they have no reason to do so," Crazy Horse said lightly.

"Can't you see how serious this is? They mean to have you out of the way. *Any way they can.*" Little Hawk broke off his empassioned argument and paced back and forth in front of Crazy Horse.

Above them the bare limbs of a cottonwood rattled like bones in a graveyard. A few desultory crows sat hunch-shouldered on the branches, bright, black eyes searching the snow-dotted ground for any morsel of food. Agitated nearly to the point of speechlessness, Little Hawk at last spoke his plan.

"They must be fooled. Deceived into thinking you are no longer here. Lend me your best robe and your shield. Some of the Raven Owners Society and I will ride out and confront them, then decoy them off after us. While we do this, you ride fast to Spotted Tail's agency and tell of the troubles to Major Lee."

"I do not run from danger," Crazy Horse said stubbornly, arms crossed over his chest.

"We all know you are a brave man. But brave men don't meekly stick their heads in the noose. Believe me, Crazy Horse, Women's Dress, Big Bat, and all the rest of that clan of villains wants to see you dead."

Somewhat mollified, Crazy Horse thought this over. "It is a strategy? Like we used against the soldiers of Yellow Hair at the Greasy Grass?" A smile flickered, faded, then firmed up into a white slash in Crazy Horse's broad, dark face. "This way it is we who will hide our laughter behind our hands. It shall be as you say, Cetanla."

Two more days passed before Women's Dress and Johnny Broughier whipped up enough enthusiasm among the idlers at the agency. They started out in high spirits. Someone produced a bottle and it went the rounds. Jokes and laughter ran along the small column. They could barely make out the glint of the Missouri in the distance when a yipping party of Oglala seemed to rise up out of the rolling prairie and ride swiftly along their flank, shouting insults.

"There, that one. It's Crazy Horse," Women's Dress shouted. "After them!"

At once the chase began. The Oglala tactic that had so often led unsuspecting soldiers to their destruction worked equally well on the rabble assembled by the plotters. Little Hawk and his companions led them further and further away from the lodges of Crazy Horse's people. Men who had not been on horseback for many months soon began to complain. A couple who had indulged of the bottle too much turned to the side and bent far over their horses' necks to vomit onto the frosted ground. Unseen by the blood-lusting party of Bad Faces, another contingent rode out from the distant village and made progress rapidly southward, toward the Spotted Tail agency, at the headwaters of the White Earth River.

Like whispering leaves on a summer's night, news traveled rapidly through the Spotted Tail agency people. Crazy Horse, along with his wife, Black Shawl, Shell Boy, Kicking Bear, and a number of his picked warriors, had come in a hurry. Rumors of trouble at Red Cloud's town came with this intelligence. Major Lee heard of it almost before Crazy Horse crossed over the boundary onto the agency.

Such a situation far from pleased him, yet he looked forward to conversing with a man of such remakable reputation. Yes, Major Lee confided to himself, he would enjoy a visit from Crazy Horse. Accordingly, he went out smiling to greet the new arrivals and welcome them. He personally escorted Crazy Horse inside the stout log building that served as the agency headquarters.

"Tell me," Lee began pleasantly in Lakota, "what brings you to visit us?"

Crazy Horse frowned in concentration. He had no set idea of what or how much to say to the friendly agent. On the three-day ride, he had considered the problem carefully and still had no clear way. At last Crazy Horse decided on simply unloading the whole story and gauging what he should do next by Lee's reaction. He licked his lower lip and proceeded with the tale.

At its conclusion, Major Lee looked at him with compassion and understanding. His words, though, hardly matched his inner feelings. "I and my family, and the families of Spotted Tail's band, would welcome you here, of course. But that is not for us to decide. Only General Bradley, or General Crook or General Miles, can rule as to where you will live. I'm sorry, Crazy Horse, but you must return to the Red Cloud agency and present your case to General Bradley. He's a fair man and he'll listen."

For long, silent minutes, Crazy Horse meditated upon what Major Lee had told him. The unease with which he had left the Red Cloud agency returned manyfold, an almost overwhelming foretaste of doom. He struggled for the words to explain this premonition to Major Lee.

"If we do this. If we go back, and the police are still looking for us, it is told me something bad will happen. Something terribly bad."

It became Lee's turn to consider the matter soberly. From Crazy Horse's standpoint, to act either way would be wrong. Damn it, the man deserved his own reservation. Circumstances had contrived to make that delayed, if not impossible. What could the Indian police have plotted against him? Questioning did no good. No matter, Crazy Horse should be kept under heavy guard until such time as Miles returned and resolved the situation. After two days of discussions, Lee at last outlined a compromise solution.

"I will escort you to the Red Cloud agency. With us will come Bordeaux, Black Crow, and Swift Bear. Also High Bear and Touch the Clouds. We will see that you are not arrested out of hand and that you get a chance to explain to General Bradley."

Crazy Horse pondered this, then grunted assent. "I agree. But only if these things are done. Neither I nor the soldier agent will take guns. General Bradley at Fort Robinson, and Colonel Clark, should be told all that we have done these past two days, especially that both Spotted Tail and you, Major Lee, have agreed to let my people live among you if the soldier-chief says it can be done."

"Yes, yes, we can agree to that," Lee replied.

"One thing more. I am to be allowed to tell the soldier-chiefs how my words at the council had been twisted by Johnny Broughier. I want them to understand I had said nothing of fighting white men. All I wanted was peace and a home for my people."

"We'll help you all we can," Major Lee responded eagerly. Spotted Tail agreed likewise.

Within a few minutes, the party was organized and started off. The group rode with light hearts. Then, fifteen miles out from Robinson, many scouts from Red Cloud's band came up. The old unease assailed Crazy Horse again. At Chadron Creek, more scouts showed themselves, until they numbered sixty. All wore the blue soldier coats. And now, riding among these, Crazy Horse knew that he was already a prisoner.

Chapter 24

Days of sunshine had banished the snow, and a fleeting hint of Indian Summer drifted through the land on a light, warm breeze. Eli Holten's spirits had healed, along with his body, by the time he reached Fort Keogh. He went at once to report to Nelson Miles.

"The civilian wagons and your artillery arrived safely at Fort Benton, General. I suppose, with the telegraph, you know that already."

"Yes, but it's nice to hear it in person. You seem chipper enough, Holten. The wounds heal properly?"

"Yes, sir. Nothing but a few lumps and scars to add to the rest. I would say your campaign was fairly well ended."

"It is, though the Nez Percé are yet to be transported south. Some are to go to Fort Lawton, in Indian Territory, others to Fort Leavenworth in Kansas. The remainder will be sent to the Nez Percé agency at Kamiah or Fort Lapwai in Idaho. It appears that White Bird managed to get into Canada after all. So, with the Nez Percé split up that way there'll never be another chance for them to band together and terrorize the countryside. Which leaves us with but one unfinished problem."

"Oh? At a guess, I'd say it's Crazy Horse."

"Exactly, Holten. I'm releasing you to return to the Twelfth at Fort Rawlins. On your way, I'd like to entrust a message to you. It's to Crazy Horse. Please tell him that I will give every help possible to the establishment of a northern agency if he is still unsatisfied with Red Cloud."

"It's rather the other way around, but your heart's in the right place. I know Crazy Horse will be pleased, General. He'll need all the help he can get."

"I'll give it unstintingly, rest assured of that. Besides, a side trip to Fort Thompson should give you a chance to see that lovely teamster with whom you're so smitten," Miles added with a wink.

" 'Smitten,' sir? I thought only old maids used that word."

"Get out of here, Holten, before I think up some other assignment for you. And by the way, you were right. It *did* snow by the first part of October."

Never had Eli Holten seen so many Indians gathered at Fort Thompson, or at any other military post for that matter. On ponies, in wagons, and on foot, the Sioux had come to stand quietly around the buildings of the military command. He puzzled at the reason as he worked his way among them and halted outside the headquarters building. In the orderly room, General Bradley's sergeant major ushered the scout inside.

"Good to see you, Holten," Bradley declared with less-than-sincere enthusiasm. "What brings you here?"

"I've a message to deliver from General Miles."

"He may have been confirmed," Bradley snapped with an acid tongue, "but he's not in grade until January, nor does he command the department as yet."

"Uh, if you'll excuse me, General, I sort of miss what that's all about. My message is for Crazy Horse."

"What! Miles has nothing to say and nothing to do with that matter."

Holten tried a light laugh. "I'm getting more confused by the moment, General Bradley. What hasn't General Miles anything to do with?"

"The issue has already been resolved. I have my orders. I'm sure you saw the influx of savages when you rode in? Well, they've come to see Crazy Horse get what's coming to him. He jumped the reservation, you see. With a war party. Then he turned yellow and gave himself up at Spotted Tail's agency. He's coming back under guard of Indian police and we're going to fix his wagon once and for all."

Instant fury blackened the scout's face. He knew better than to remark too strongly over a decision of army higher-ups, yet he longed to smash a fist into the arrogant, sneering face in front of him. With an effort he bridled his rage and spoke softly.

"I'm reminded of an old adage a mountain man told me: 'You can cheat an Indian once and get away with it. But don't try it again, and never, never lie to one.'"

"Well, that's all academic now, isn't it. There'll be no need for you to deliver your message. I'll see that you're allotted quarters for one night, Holten, then I expect to see you on your way. Now, good day."

That officious, self-important son of a bitch, Holten thought angrily as he stalked out of the office. Despite his black mood, he noted that the crowd had grown considerably. A short distance away, Eli recognized He Dog. The young warrior led his best charger and had a far-off cast to his eyes.

216

"Sunkbloka, here is Tall Bear."

"I see you, Tall Bear," He Dog answered.

"Is it true that Crazy Horse is under arrest?"

"That is what is said around here. I'm not so sure. I will ride out and meet him."

"Take him my regards as a friend."

"He'll like that."

He Dog mounted and raced away. Several minutes passed and a roar went up from the far edge of the crowd. Holten made out the large cavalcade that approached at a slow trot. When they grew nearer, he recognized Crazy Horse, riding in the center, with He Dog at his side. Crazy Horse wore a dark blue shirt and leggings, with a single eagle feather in the braid of his light brown hair. He carried no weapons and no shield. To Holten, he looked frightfully alone. The party had no sooner halted outside the headquarters building than Little Big Man came strutting up with all the self-importance of a leader of the Indian police. He grabbed Crazy Horse by one arm and jerked him around.

"Come along, you man of no-fight. You are a coward!"

To Holten's surprise, the great Oglala let the insult pass with no remark. Rather, he went quietly into the offices with the men from the ambulance that had accompanied the column. Holten noted the presence of Major Lee, Bordeaux, Black Crow, and Swift Bear. By now the crowd had separated into factions, Holten observed.

The few who were still Crazy Horse warriors filled spaces between many buildings. On the other side the agency scouts, with Red Cloud and American Horse at their heads, gathered to glower at their imagined rivals. Nowhere did he see sign of Woman's Dress, Grabber, or White Hat. Nor was Spotted Tail there,

though many of his Brules had apparently accompa
nied Crazy Horse this far. As the outer door closed
Holten heard Lee talking to Crazy Horse.

"You wait here, Crazy Horse, with the others. I'l
go in and talk to General Bradley."

With a reassuring handshake and nod, Lee de
parted. He entered the office and came directly to th
point. After an impassioned presentation of th
wrongs he believed had been done to Crazy Horse, h
waited for a response from his superior. Bradley
surveyed him a moment, lips curled in distaste fo
anyone who would champion one of those savages
At last he delivered his fateful blow.

"All most interesting, Major. Unfortunately, noth
ing can be done any more."

"Nothing? Then . . . it's really very bad?"

"Yes," Bradley agreed. "Very bad. Not even Crook
can change the orders I've received. Not a hair on th
chief's head is to be harmed, but he must now b
turned over to the officer of the day to be confined
Say to him that it is too late to have a talk."

It was a dismissal, which Lee took badly. Still
putting on a good face, he went out to Crazy Horse
"I have told him everything that you wanted con
veyed, Crazy Horse. He heard it in all seriousness
Now he must think on it. Night is nearly on us an
General Bradley said it was too late for talking. Fo
now you are to go with the little soldier-chief and yo
will not be harmed."

"*Hau!*" Crazy Horse replied, willing to cooperat
now in hope his pleas would at last be heard an
acted upon.

He extended his hand and exchanged a friendl
shake with Lee, grateful for his assistance. He the
shook hands with the officer of the day, who starte
for the door. When it opened, Holten saw Craz

Horse between the OOD and Little Big Man, with two soldiers behind. Some of the agency Indians hurried on ahead of the party, as though they knew exactly where to go. As they crossed to another building, one Holten knew only too well, the warriors and scouts pushed in toward each other and raised such a noise that it became a roar. Under it, from all quarters, Eli heard the click of guns cocking. Crazy Horse excelled all the others for quiet dignity.

His blanket folded over his arm as though he were going to his lodge between two friends, the Oglala chief let himself be taken past a soldier who walked up and down with a bayoneted rifle on his shoulder, and in through a door. Holten groaned at the sight of it. Only after he had entered did Crazy Horse see the barred windows and the men with chains on their legs.

Immediately he recognized it as the dread Iron House.

Holten heard the dreaded noise from inside as Crazy Horse instantly jumped back, with a cry of dismay, and drew a hidden gift knife to strike out around him. Little Big Man grabbed his arms from behind. In an attempt to break free, Crazy Horse struggled into the open, dragging Little Big Man with him. At once a cry went up from Crazy Horse's loyal warriors.

"He is holding the arms, the arms!"

On the other side, the scouts raised their guns as Red Cloud and American Horse ordered, "Shoot in the middle; shoot to kill!"

Leaping fearlessly into the middle of this fray, the officer of the day knocked down the scout guns with his sword as fast as they came up. And between them, the great Oglala plunged to get free, growling,

"Let me go! Let me go!" His knife flashed in the evening sun. Then, with a mighty jerk, Crazy Horse threw himself sideways and Little Big Man had to drop one hand, blood running from a slash across his arm.

Holten looked on in fascinated helplessness as Swift Bear and other Brule friendlies grabbed Crazy Horse in an attempt to get the melee stopped. To their misfortune, the enraged OOD stepped in, slashing with his sword.

"Stab him!" he yelled. "Kill the son of a bitch!"

The stockade guard came running up and lunged with his bayonet. His aimed proved untrue and he buried the long steel shaft in the door. Swiftly he jerked the weapon free and lunged twice more. At a grisly redness on the steel, a noise of alarm, one of warning, rose from the watching Sioux. Crazy Horse pulled at his old captors once more.

"Let me go, my friends," he panted. "You have got me hurt enough."

Stunned by these soft words, all the Indians suddenly dropped their hands from Crazy Horse as though terribly afraid. Several turned away in shame. Released, Crazy Horse staggered backward, turned half around. Through the tear-filled eyes of a fourteen-year-old suffering under the long-ago sun, Eli Holten saw his once-hero sink to the ground, his shirt and leggings wet and blood-darkened. He heard a sob and only tardily realized it came from his own throat.

Silently the mob dissolved, leaving the dying man alone in the dirt.

Eli Holten didn't wait to keep the grim vigil. He grained and saddled Sonny, replaced a few supplies in is saddlebags, and rode out of Fort Thompson choked with fury and grief. Behind him, still glowing with the overwhelming pride of being the man who "fixed Crazy Horse for good," General Bradley refused the request of friends and his own post surgeon that Crazy Horse be allowed to be taken to his own lodge to die. Instead he relented only in that the dying Oglala could be placed in the adjutant's office instead of the guardhouse.

Holten knew none of this, though, as he cantered off in his bitterness. He had shared the grief of Joseph's defeat and now this. In such sorry ends as these, neither side won. Only evil seemed to triumph. And the only songs to be sung would be the mourning of the women, red and white, for the loss of ones early loved and frightfully gone.

Why? For what good purpose had it all been done? Eli Holten, like so many others that night, wondered on it as he turned Sonny's nose to the east, toward Fort Rawlins. Perhaps there he would find an answer, or at least peace, and an end to the visions that haunted him.

THE UNTAMED WEST
brought to you by Zebra Books

THE LAST MOUNTAIN MAN (1480, $2.2?)
by William W. Johnstone

He rode out West looking for the men who murdered his fathe
and brother. When an old mountain man taught him how to kill
man a hundred different ways from Sunday, he knew he'd mak
sure they all remembered . . . THE LAST MOUNTAIN MAN.

SAN LOMAH SHOOTOUT (1853, $2.5?)
by Doyle Trent

Jim Kinslow didn't even own a gun, but a group of hardcase
tried to turn him into buzzard meat. There was only one way t
find out why anybody would want to stretch his hide out to dr
and that was to strap on a borrowed six-gun and ride to death ?
glory.

TOMBSTONE LODE (1915, $2.9?)
by Doyle Trent

When the Josey mine caved in on Buckshot Dobbs, he left behin
a rich vein of Colorado gold—but no will. James Alexande
hired to investigate Buckshot's self-proclaimed blood relatio?
learns too soon that he has one more chance to solve the myste?
and save his skin or become another victim of TOMBSTON
LODE.

GALLOWS RIDERS (1934, $2.5?)
by Mark K. Roberts

When Stark and his killer-dogs reached Colby, all it took wa?
little muscle and some well-placed slugs to run roughshod ov
the small town—until the avenging stranger stepped out of t?
shadows for one last bloody showdown.

DEVIL WIRE (1937, $2.5?)
by Cameron Judd

They came by night, striking terror into the hearts of the settle?
The message was clear: Get rid of the devil wire or the land wou?
turn red with fencestringer blood. It was the beginning of a bru?
range war.

Available wherever paperbacks are sold, or order direct from t
Publisher. Send cover price plus 50¢ per copy for mailing a?
handling to Zebra Books, Dept. 2149, 475 Park Avenue Sou?
New York, N.Y. 10016. Residents of New York, New Jersey a?
Pennsylvania must include sales tax. DO NOT SEND CASH.

WHITE SQUAW
Zebra's Adult Western Series
by E.J. Hunter

Available wherever paperbacks are sold, or order direct from the publisher. Send cover price plus 50¢ per copy for mailing and handling to Zebra Books, Dept. 2149, 475 Park Avenue South, New York, N.Y. 10016. DO NOT SEND CASH.